MW00647824

A STONE OF DESTINY AND DESPAIR

THE LEVANTHRIA SERIES
BOOK FOUR

A.P BESWICK

Edited By - Quinn Nichols, Quill and Bone Editing

Cover Design - Rafido

ISBN - 978-1-916671-06-5

THE LEGENDS OF LEVANTHRIA

To The Legends Of Levanthria who have supported each of the books in the series so far on Kickstarter.
Thank you

The Merry Men.... And Women
Seth (The Little) Alexander
Joshua (The Scarlett) Gray
Daniel (The Friar)
Dorman Robin (The Hood) Hill

The Legendary Pieces Of Eight
Seth (Blackbeard) Alexander
Z (The Sparrow)

THE LEGENDS OF LEVANTHRIA

The Dragon

Louis Jay Dombroski

Jen Smith

Zaakir (The Archer) Patel

Sunny Side Up

Señor Neo

Jacob Salm

Rhonda K Koenning

Brandon H Beers

Jeremiah Silva

Seth Alexander

Christopher Simard

Matthew Schaaff

Armin Enjoyer of Well Written Books

Damien Troutman

Meredith Carstens

Tanya Hagel

Michael William

Alexander Gonser

THE LEGENDS OF LEVANTHRIA

The Dragon

Andrew Sheridan

Ian White

Geoff Seutter

R. S. Howell

Brian R Knoblich

Kevin Camps

Benjamin Powell

Oliver Stegmann

Lauren O'Connor

Travis Hawkins

Joshua Gray

Troy Hauck, RN

Kat Holder

Christian Mays

Dominic Jones

Charlotte Lotte de Reuver

Valerie Wiechmann and Shane Libihoul

Forest of Opiya

Pendaren Hill

Eltera

Gondoron Pass

Askela

Osar

Levanthria

Literian Plains

Uster

f Antar

Yugo's Tears

N

Rivah

Voraz

Zakron Keep

A STONE OF DESTINY AND DESPAIR

I

LAITH

"King Athos Almerion is dead, Levanthria is in turmoil as the King had no heir to ascend the throne. This is unprecedented as the King also had no siblings, his bloodline effectively ending with him."

LETTER to the court of Byron, Coratious Vex, 255 KR

"COME ON OLD MAN, KEEP UP!" I call back to Jordell who trails behind, the steep hills of Pendara proving a difficult obstacle for my resolute friend.

"Less of the old man," Jordell calls back. "In my day if I spoke to someone like that, I would have received a whack to the back of my head." His face reads like a map, wrinkled and worn. His robe trails across scorched grass on the hills, a sign that this region is in the midst of a drought.

The sun is relentless. Heat enters my lungs as I breathe, making the hike up this hill more uncomfortable than I would have liked. Sweat beads on my head and my tunic is sodden. Given that I have been unable to bathe for well past a week now, I fear that my smell has become unfavourable.

"How much farther must we hike in this heat?" I ask, stopping to let Jordell regain some ground on me.

It takes him a few moments, but the man is determined. "We should be near. I have not visited this house for many years," Jordell says. He stops beside me to gather his breath, sweat pooling under his darkened eyes. His chest rattles as he wheezes.

"We need to rest," I tell him. "That chest of yours is getting worse." Maybe when we reach our destination, he will for once heed my words. It has been a long journey across Levanthria, since our return from foreign lands. We had to travel slowly, without drawing attention to ourselves. Afterall, Morgana has put a high bounty on our heads alongside Vireo, apparent on the notices we have seen scattered across these lands.

"Nonsense, boy. There is still daylight. We can rest when we reach the Redfearn house." He smiles before setting off once more. "Although this would be an easier journey had you not lost our horses."

"I told you that wasn't my fault! I swear I tied them properly. Someone took them, I'm sure of it," I protest, but I know my words fall on deaf ears.

I have no idea where Jordell gets his energy from. He is relentless in his pursuit of learning about the artefact that has us traipsing through the countryside: a sword embedded deep within a body of stone, its steel fused with its casing, unmoved for thousands of years. Jordell told me of it not long after we left Askela but in the years that have passed since then, we have unturned no clues as to its whereabouts. We have travelled across Levanthria, attending different temples and libraries in search of anything that could point us in the right direction.

I would be lying if I said I had not questioned the sword's existence on more than a few occasions in the years since we left the Forest of Opiya. But if war is coming, one that hinges on the very sword we search for, I need to be ready so that I can help protect the people of Levanthria. I feel duty bound with the knowledge that the sword could be real. It is why I follow Jordell, it is why I learn from him and train with him every opportunity I get.

"Tell me, Jordell, if this next destination leads to nothing, are we to move on to a new quest?" I have gone everywhere the wizard has asked, done everything I have needed to, trained every single day. And yet, we have found nothing.

"You do show your age with your youthful need to complete everything at speed, Laith. Sometimes it is the journey we make, the roads that lead us there, that help us become the person we need to be. Perhaps in time, you will learn that this could be seen as the quest, not the item that we seek to find." He continues steadfast, trailing his leg behind him with a slight limp he has carried since rescuing Lek's leg in the Forest of Opiya. A feat he more than likely regrets given that ogre's betrayal. One from which I still bear the scars.

Jordell stops and stretches out his arm, unfurling his hand until his finger points in the direction of a small stone house. The broken thatched roof has seen better days. Sections of it are charred, and the chimney is crumbling.

"We are here," Jordell announces proudly.

"Where exactly is here?" I ask. The ramshackle house I look at is not exactly what I envisioned for the three powerful witches.

"This is where the Redfearn sisters reside, three witches who are connected to Elven blood, although looking at the house it appears it may have seen better days." Jordell cuts a concerned expression and paces up the hill as if his advanced years have turned back time. I struggle to keep up my stride with his.

When we reach the house, it is clear that something has happened here. The windows are smashed, the door hangs limply off its hinges, and the ground around it is painted with tar in a strange, star-like symbol.

"To ward off demons," Jordell explains, examining the symbol further. "Briasse? Lyrissa? Zerina?"

"I don't think anyone is here." I poke my head through the doorway. The house smells of damp and mould, and the air is musty from where water has trickled in from a hole in the roof. "This place has been ransacked," I add.

When I step inside, glass crunches underfoot, the rotting floorboards squelching as I move into the house. "Now are you going to finally tell me what exactly it is that you need from here?"

Jordell examines the inside of the house, his wrinkled face perplexed as he ponders on his thoughts. "Briasse, the eldest of the sisters, used to visit me at the Great Temple in Askela. She needed help with her sister, Lyrissa, who had succumbed to an affliction of overusing her magic. She spoke of a book, one that contained Elven rituals that her mother had passed onto her, one that I was hoping may have been in this house."

"We already have a rare spellbook. What do we need Elven magic for?" I ask, annoyed to discover that Jordell has dragged us all the way to the northeastern lands of Levanthria for nothing but a few words on a page.

"Elven magic is more powerful than any other. I have studied the spellbook we have from front to back ten times over. While my magic has grown in power, there is still more to be learned. If we can find the book Briasse spoke of, it may have information on powerful artefacts."

Jordell opens a cupboard and sighs with frustration when it falls from its hinges and clatters onto the ground. "I fear for what has happened here, and for the sisters' fates." He stares out the window for a moment whilst collecting his thoughts. "Interesting."

"What?"

Jordell pushes past me and heads outside into the barren fields of the Pendaran Hills.

"Jordell," I call after him, but he is oblivious to my words. With no option, I follow him outside as he moves across the dried grass. He drops to his knees and bows his head to the ground.

"I am sorry," I hear his muttered words.

In front of him sits two small piles of rocks.

"Graves?" I ask.

"They are in good condition. I think they were formed recently."

"May I ask what it is you are doing by my sisters' graves?" a voice demands from behind us.

I spin to see a ghostly pale woman standing in front of the house. Her long, jet-black hair hangs loosely over her shoulders and down her back, the wind blowing it to one side. She wears a tricorn hat and a long black overcoat. She grips the hilt of her sword as if she is ready to attack.

"Whoa." I raise my hands in the air. "We want no quarrel with you. My friend here wished only to visit those who lived here."

"How do you know of us?" The woman draws her sword and points it at me.

"I suggest you answer her!" A man steps from around the side of the house, unsheathing his sword without hesitation, as though he relishes a fight. There is an aggressiveness to his tone that matches his frowning expression. He is also dressed for the seas, with his tricorn hat and long brown jacket. A thick, black beard covers his face.

Jordell looks the pair up and down, studying them both intently. "Zerina, is that you?" he asks. "My name is Jordell. I was a friend to Briasse." He slowly steps towards her, his hands far out in front of him to show he means no harm.

"Take another step and I will gut you where you stand!" the man speaks through gritted teeth.

"It is okay, Ulrik, I do not think this man wishes us harm." The woman reaches out and gently presses on the tip of the man's outstretched blade until it points at the ground.

"Zerina, we have been stung before, I do not see why we should take the risk with these people." The man stands firm, but his partner stands even firmer. She stares into his eyes and the two exchange a look before the man reluctantly resheathes his weapon. His aggression emits from every part of him; his breathing is short and sharp, his muscles taut with adrenaline. This person wants a fight.

I place my hand on the hilt of my sword.

"Calm, Ulrik, I am certain we can call these men our friends," Zerina says. "Jordell, you say? My sister did speak of you." She walks towards Jordell and stands before him, searching his eyes. Then, she wraps her arms around him and hugs him tightly, as a child would their father.

Jordell appears taken aback by this. He gently pats her on her back and the two share a tender moment. It is strange to see such genuine comfort being drawn from two people that have only just met, and I stand awkwardly, keeping my eyes on Ulrik, who still seems as though he is spoiling for a fight.

"Briasse told me she was in possession of a book that contains ancient Elven rituals. We are trying to find something that could turn the tides of this war and finally bring an age of peace and prosperity across Levanthria. I am so sorry for your loss, Zerina, truly I am."

"Come inside, we have much to discuss." Zerina guides Jordell back towards the house, placing her hand delicately on his arm as they walk.

"Have you not heard news of the king?" Ulrik growls.

"What of him?" I ask, curious as to the sudden turn of the conversation.

"I killed him."

2

JORDELL

L aith looked just as shocked as I felt. It couldn't be true.
And yet, as soon as Ulrik speaks the words, I know he
does not lie: King Athos Almerion is dead.

"What do you mean? King Athos is dead?" Laith demands
as we re-enter the house.

I give Laith a warning glance for his tone. I've watched the
green-eyed boy grow into a formidable young man, with his
athletic build and dirty-blond hair. But he still has much to
learn.

Ulrik throws some logs into the hearth and lights a fire
with a piece of flint. A small flame ignites and Ulrik places
some kindling over the top. He remains concentrated on the
flames, apparently uninterested in answering Laith's question.

"How has this come to be, Zerina?" I ask. "If this is true and
King Athos is dead, this could change the landscape of Levanthria." My mind searches over the vision I shared with the
sorceress Morgana all those years ago. The king was not
present in it, despite there being a great war. Is this something
that the gods have prophesied that I've remained blind to?

Zerina rummages around the dining space and pulls up two stools, passing them to Laith and me. The stools are frail and damp, mould creeping up their legs like an infection over a wound. I wonder for a moment if it will stand the test of bearing my weight, but Laith does not hesitate to take a seat. It was some walk to get to the top of these hills, after all, and we are not yet rested. Laith lets out a sigh of relief as he takes the burden of the plains off his feet. When I see that it does not collapse beneath him, it at least gives me enough confidence to do the same.

Zerina takes a seat, casting her eyes over Ulrik, her face a picture of concern and worry for her friend. The man now seems lost as he stares into the growing flames of the fire.

"Is it a bad thing?" Zerina says. "Is the king dying really that bad? Look at the state of Levanthria, look at the state in which he has left things. My sisters and I were dragged away to the witch trials because the king demanded that those who bear magic were to be enlisted to fight his war. When we declined, my sisters were slaughtered like animals."

"So, you did it in revenge for killing your sisters?" I ask, still in disbelief that somehow these two were responsible for the death of the king.

"No!" Zerina says sharply. "I swore an oath to protect my companion. It is they who sought revenge against the king." Zerina holds a prolonged stare over Ulrik once more, tears welling in her eyes as she speaks. "We lost someone special to both of us, and it hit them harder than I could ever imagine." Zerina takes a deep breath as if being mindful of the words that she speaks. The crackling in the fire grows louder as warmth finally starts to greet us. "Ulrik, he was a good man – he *is* a good man," she corrects herself before wiping away her tears with the back of her hand.

I consider asking her who it was they lost, but the anguish

9

in her eyes stops me. The burden she carries from the death of her sisters must be unbearable, enough to break anyone. To then add further loss and grief to that...

"The king got what he fucking deserved." Ulrik's voice is gravelly like sandpaper. He raises both of his hands in front of the fire, embracing the heat. "Everything that happened was because of him. Think of all the lives that have been destroyed because of his actions. At least now he cannot cause any more damage to these lands. I only wish to be in that position again so that I could savour the moment that he took his final breath, one last time. Enjoy every passing second that he endured when the blast ripped through his stomach."

"And what of the aftermath? What events will now befall Levanthria once word of his death spreads?" Laith asks.

"Ulrik had no desire or intention to worry about the aftermath of their actions. They have been driven by a vow of revenge since we left the island of Treventine," Zerina explains. She glances at Ulrik once more with a look somewhere between apprehension, concern, and exasperation. "I only hope that they will finally find peace now that they have fulfilled their blood oath. I fear for what grief has done to their mind." There is a paternalistic way that Zerina speaks about Ulrik, which I find quite strange given their similar age and shared experiences. I wonder if the two of them are lovers but the bond they appear to share is more in keeping of that of a brother and sister.

"Treventine?" I muse. "To tread such treacherous waters will have been no easy feat. What was it that took you there?"

"A map, and a vision from my murdered sister. That, however, is a story for another time, Jordell. Our boat lies to the east of these hills. We merely made port so I could finally make graves for my sisters. It has taken us weeks to return from the eastern lands of Horath."

Horath, I know, is where King Athos Almerion has been for the last seven years fighting his war against the Zarubians. What a fool's war it has proven to be, with only his ego serving him and motivating to keep up the battle front. His desire to quell enemies before they have even shown, let alone declared, their intention to invade Levanthria.

"The vision I shared with Morgana . . . it is the king's death that led to the aftermath. I am certain of it. This is what brings us to your home, Zerina. It must be fated that you should be here at the moment we arrived."

"What exactly are you here for, mage?"

"Please, I am not a mage. I will not cast magic to cause any harm. I use it only to aid and protect others." My reply is hard like stone. I do not want to be associated with the kind of destructive magic that mages possess.

"We will need to find another name for you, then," Zerina answers curiously. "You still haven't answered my question, Jordell."

"A book. Your sister, Briasse, told me about a book written in Elvish that spoke of great artefacts. Would you to happen to know the location of that book, or even confirm to me that such a book exists?"

Zerina casts her curious eyes over me once more. She is hesitant to answer at first but after a brief pause, she does. "You aided my sister when we had no one else to turn to. Briasse clearly trusted you and I sense no darkness in you." Her eyes flicker from me to Laith, the crackling fire and stifled breaths the only noise for an awkward moment. "Wait here." Zerina stands from her stool and heads to a room at the far side of the ransacked house. The broken glass and plates crunch under her feet as she disappears.

"Do you think we will learn where to find this sword?" Laith asks. "Do you think this will bring forth your visions?"

"I feel that I must be careful with the visions of which you speak. They could be misleading. How they play out in life could be a matter of interpretation, like choosing a side on a battlefield. No doubt both armies feel they are fighting for the right cause."

An uncomfortable squeak of scraping wood causes the hairs on my arm to stand as Zerina moves things around in one of the rooms. She curses as something heavy crashes onto the floor.

"There it is," I hear her say. Zerina exits the room with something in her hands bound in what would have been white cloth. It is now stained with dirt, but has done its job of protecting whatever lies inside.

"Ulrik, the table." Zerina nods towards the overturned table by the broken window. Ulrik quickly moves from the fire and Laith helps him lift the heavy oak table and place it upright.

Zerina lays the item down and stares blankly at it. "In truth, I have not seen this tome since my mother passed. She gave it to Briasse before she was taken from us." Her eyes began to well once more as her memories trace over her past. A single teardrop falls from her cheek and lands on the dust-covered table, leaving a strange splash mark as it becomes one with the dirt.

"Are you okay?" Ulrik asks, placing a hand on Zerina's shoulder.

"It draws my thoughts to all that I have lost." Zerina delicately unwraps the cloth that protects the tome.

I wait with tentative anticipation of what lies within. My spirits lift when I see a leather-bound book in near perfect condition. Gilded lettering and symbols that I recognise as Elvish adorn the cover, a circular emblem filled with hieroglyphics etched on the outer edge. Zerina blows off what dust has settled on the cover of the book before wiping away the rest with a gentle brush of her hand.

"I presume this is what you are searching for?" she says.

I feel my eyes widen with anticipation. For years our efforts have borne no fruits. We have travelled most of Levanthria in search of learning more about the sacred stone that I have foreseen. I can only hope that within this ancient book lies the answers that we seek. I am certain that the very future of Levanthria depends on it.

Zerina slowly turns the pages, which seem too thick to be made of paper.

"May I?" I ask.

Zerina nods and steps to one side. I skim over the first page, but I cannot fully decipher the Elvish words even after transcribing my own spellbook. Turning the page, the texture feels strange, as if it is formed from some kind of hide. The smell of rich leather drifts over me, combined with the mustiness only brought about through age and damp. I can't begin to think how old this book may be. Each page I turn carries symbols and words that I do not know the meaning of, but intricate drawings and sketches are contained within. I pore over the contents, entranced by diagrams of waterfalls, the ocean, caves. I reach one that contains a near full-page drawing of a tree. Its branches stretch out above the stars that sit at the top of the page. Underneath, there are multiple symbols that I cannot decipher. My heart sinks.

"The tree of life," Zerina mutters under her breath.

"You can read these?" I ask in wonderment. "How? How did you come to be able to read such ancient scriptures?"

"We found the waters long hidden by the Elves. When it washed over me, it cleansed me of the burden of my magic-use and granted me knowledge you could not begin to fathom." Zerina's face becomes sorrowful as she speaks. "But it came at a price, leaving us with nothing but anger and grief." She places her hand on the crisp, ancient pages as if she draws comfort from them. "We lost nearly all our crew. One of our men, Orjan . . . he helped us activate the water's true power."

"Orjan?" Laith interjects. "Was he of Rashouya?"

"Why yes, yes he was," Zerina says, taken aback. "You know of him?"

"I was his squire," Laith answers, his voice elevated. It is a name I have not heard him speak of for some time, yet I can see it still pulls at him like a fish on a line.

"When we came across him, we thought him nothing but a drunk, but I soon learned he possessed courage that not many in these lands carry." Zerina swallows hard, as if her mouth fills with oil.

"Please, you must tell me his whereabouts," Laith asks in desperation, rushing beside Zerina and placing his hand at the side of the spellbook. "I need to know that he is okay."

"That he is now," Ulrik snarls, tossing some kindling into the fire. "He deserves his curse."

"His curse?" Laith asks.

Judging by the venom on Ulrik's tongue, it is clear to me that something serious has happened between him and Orjan, and I feel it wise not to poke him with further questions. It does, however, cause a pang of frustration in me that Orjan still has a hold on Laith's heart, despite the fact that Orjan abandoned Laith when the boy needed him most.

Zerina places her hand on top of Laith's. "Orjan bore the brunt of a curse that needed to be triggered so that we could use the waters within Traventine."

"What happened to him? Is he okay? Where is he now?" Laith eyes dart from Zerina to Ulrik as he struggles with what he hears.

"At least he is alive," Ulrik speaks through gritted teeth. "Unlike my brother, whose life he took."

"No!" Laith protests. "Orjan is no cold-blooded murderer, I can't—"

"Ulrik!" Zerina scolds before turning her attention back to Laith. "He is alive, or least he was when we left him. What Ulrik says is true." She casts Ulrik a scowl, who waves her disapproval away like he is swatting a fly. "An ancient Elven curse has caused his form to change, and for him to lose his mind."

"What do you mean, caused his form to change?"

"He became disfigured," Zerina answers. "His appearance, his body was cracked, his mind broken as he was transformed into a lizard-man. He attacked us. With my magic, I was able to free his mind from the curse, but even with the knowledge that the waters granted me, I could not reverse the disfigurement. Orjan eventually left us. He bore the pain of ending the life of someone we both held dear, and he couldn't bear to be around us anymore, despite my protests."

"I couldn't be held responsible for what I would have done, had he stayed," Ulrik says. "My only regret is not ending his miserable life for him."

"Where?" Laith asks. "Where is it you left him?"

"To the southwest of Levanthria, east of Loch Bragoah. There is an unknown cove there."

"When?"

"That was nearly three years ago," Zerina says.

Before I have any chance to comfort Laith, he stumbles backwards. "I – I need some air." He turns to leave and exits as quickly as he can. I want to follow him, but I think it wise to allow him a few moments to process everything that has just been said.

"He just needs some time," I tell the others. "Before we go, is there anything else in the book that you can translate, anything which may aid us?"

Zerina pores back over the pages and places a finger lightly on one of the symbols, a bird sitting atop a branch. "This means 'new growth'." She then traces her finger to the symbol next to it, which contains a leaf with a single horizontal line above and below. "This means 'new life'. That combined with the diagram of the tree means . . ."

"This is the Elder Tree?" My heart starts to race with excitement. "Zerina, do you know what this means?" I grew up being told stories about the tree from which life itself originated. If the diagram is here, maybe it is not merely a story.

I turn the page, my hand trembling. We have searched for so long and it feels as though we have never been closer. My chest almost bursts when my eyes land on the next page and I let out a gasp.

"What is it?" Zerina asks.

"It is here, what we have been searching for all these years." My voice shakes as I speak. A lump builds in my throat, my mouth drying in an instant.

The next page contains another diagram. This time, it is of a plinth carved from the side of a mountain – with the hilt of a sword protruding from the side.

3

LAITH

Jordell has spoken of a sword embedded in stone, but I have come to take his ramblings as nothing short of a wild errand, given the lack of progress we have made over the years.

Until now.

To see the image in this ancient Elven book all but confirms to me what Jordell has professed for so long: the magical sword, encased in stone, does exist.

Jordell updates me once I have calmed, his desperation to find the sword matched by my internal need to find Orjan. It is why I feel so conflicted. I have followed Jordell for the last three years with no evidence of the sword's existence other than his vision.

Now all I can think of is Orjan, his whereabouts, if he is okay. With no knowledge of where he is, I know it would be foolish for me to leave in search of him, but the temptation to do so rakes over my thoughts.

Choosing to remain focused on our task at hand, no matter

how difficult, I walk over to the book and take a look for myself.

"What does it say?" I ask, unable to gather any meaning from the hieroglyphs that sit underneath the diagram.

Zerina traces her hand over the symbols, speaking aloud as she reads them. "Only the chosen can call upon the power set within stone. One who will unite the kingdoms and bring about a new age of prosperity."

"This is it, Zerina." Jordell looks as excited as a child being given a gift. "This is what we have been searching for all these years. Unite the kingdoms . . . is this a prophecy?"

"It would seem so, Jordell," Zerina says.

"Does it contain any more detail?" he asks without hesitation. "We must know where it is, we must find it."

"Be careful, Jordell. If such a blade exists, there must be a reason why it remains hidden." Zerina turns the page of the book.

"But this is what I have seen, I have seen a great battle, I have seen this sword buried in the side of stone. I believe this is what will end the Great War that is coming. I believe this is how we stop Morgana."

"Morgana?" I ask. Has everything we have done been so that Jordell can bring an end to a sorceress?

"Yes, Morgana," Jordell answers. "The king is dead by Ulrik's hand. That is going to change the landscape of Levanthria. Whilst in an even weaker state, I believe Morgana is going to make a play to seize power. I believe it is her who initiates the Great War that is to come. After all, this is the vision that I shared with her."

"What if that is a manipulation on her part?" I ask. "We can't rule that out, Jordell."

"I saw the look in her eyes, Laith. When our weapons crossed on the battlefield in Askela, we shared the same vision. Somehow in that moment, our minds connected, our magic connected. I believe she sees things before anyone else. For some reason the gods grant her this and she wields it to her advantage. Such power cannot be in the hands of one person. Look at the things she has already done. Look at what happened at the Great Temple." Jordell hesitates for a moment and becomes lost in his own memories. No doubt he is reminded of the souls lost when they were sealed up in the temple without a hope of survival.

"That was Jareb who ordered that," I protest.

"But who stood by his side? You forget I knew Morgana when she was cast out of the Order. I know the manipulative skills she possesses. She will not stop until she has the power that she desires." He turns to Zerina. "Can you translate more? What else does the book say?"

The desire for knowledge seems to reach desperation for Jordell. I have never seen him like this before, and I am not sure I like it.

"It is linked to the Elder Tree, but it is not clear why," Zerina continues. "It says that the two lie opposite each other separated by the ocean. That when one greets the other, this is what will release their true power. *Fehrai*." She says the word but it means nothing to me. Zerina thinks on this for a moment. "Opiya. *Fehrai* translates to Opiya."

"The goddess?" I ask. Even I know that the Goddess Opiya was worshipped as a bringer of life. "What about the Forest of Opiya? Could it be there?" I feel proud at my own deductions from the scribing of this ancient Elven tome.

"*Zehrai*," Zerina says. "Zakron. Two points, opposite the ocean. If it does exist, the Elder Tree sits within the Forest of Opiya. I believe the stone you search for is somewhere within Zakron's Keep."

Zakron's Keep, I think to myself. "I have never heard of such a place."

"Zakron is a long-forgotten god. Erased from the books the Elves scribed millennia ago. With good reason, too." Zerina closes the book and wraps it in the cloth once more. "Jordell, if this sword has anything to do with Zakron, you must heed my warning. I fear the power that this sword could bring the bearer."

"But I have seen it, in a flash of flames, a great battle followed by peace and prosperity."

"But at what cost?" Zerina asks.

I can't help but feel as though we are going around in circles with this conversation, but I have never seen such conviction etched into Jordell's face. "What now?" I ask.

"I think we need to pay our friends a visit who find their camp in the very forest we read about."

"Vireo?"

"Maybe after all these years, they will know more."

"What about you two?" I ask Zerina. Ulrik continues to remain stony faced, as though he could erupt in a fit of rage at any moment. "If you are responsible for the king's death, you will be seen as traitors to the Crown. You are the Kingslayer. Such a title will only grant a certain death if you are captured."

"The Crown was already our enemy before we chose to sail along this path," Ulrik growls. "Let them come, let them try and take their revenge." He slams his fist into the old oak table, and I fear that the legs may break under the force.

"Even still, it would be foolish to look for the fight," I tell him. I have no affinity for the king, given everything that the people of Levanthria have endured in his absence. But I do hold a concern for what will befall the people in such uncertain times. After all, King Athos has no heir to take his throne.

"I would suggest you two lie as low as possible for a while,"

Jordell says, his eyes blinking from the dust that circles us. "When the time comes, and I believe it will not be too far from now, can we call on you to assist us in the war that is to come?"

"If it is against the rule of those that continue to inflict suffering across these lands, then aye, you have my blade and my word," Ulrik swears.

"You have my word too, Jordell. Just be careful. Our intention is to sail to Voraz. They would not be foolish enough to send any of the King's Fleet . . ." Zerina pauses. "The Royal Fleet to those shores," she corrects herself. "We will stay out of trouble there and trade our wares. If you need us, send word and we shall come."

"Thank you, Zerina. I feel that we will need as many allies as we can muster in this quest. We still have much to do but it gives me reassurance knowing that we have your swords." Jordell shakes hands with the two of them and I seek to do the same. Zerina gives a soft shake, but Ulrik responds with a much firmer grip, as though he is trying harder than he needs to. I find his efforts strange.

"Come, Laith, we must make haste." Jordell does not waste any time in setting off and heads out the front door, leaving me with no option but to quickly follow.

"Goodbye, Zerina, Ulrik." I cast the two of them a polite nod. Outside, the brightness contrasts against the darkness of the home, and it takes me a moment to gather my bearings. Fresh air greets me which is a welcome reprieve from the smell of smouldering flames and dampness. Ahead of us lies the steep decline to the foot of the Pendaran Hills.

Jordell stands tall, looking out over the hills that fall below us. "We have a long journey ahead of us, Laith. I fear that despite our years on the road, we are only just at the beginning."

I trust Jordell with my life. He has taught me so much over

the years, and I would follow him into the afterlife if I had to. But I can't help but feel that our priorities have diverged. The more I think about Orjan, the more I long to find him, to know that he is okay.

I can only pray that Jordell knows what he is doing.

4

JORDELL

" $\mathcal{I}$ have come to find that I am heralded by the town and
villages where I set foot into. If only they knew the darkness
that plagues my mind, the things I have had to do to
combat the very demons that I hunt."

JOURNAL ENTRY OF GREGOR YERALD, 102 KR

MY AGEING LEGS grow tired from the descent, but I push
through the pain at a quickened pace, motivated by the details
uncovered within Zerina's codex. On the second afternoon
since leaving the peak of the Pendaran Hills, we reach the
bottom. I let out a sigh of relief as I perch on a rock and take
out a parcel of some mushrooms that I foraged on the way
down. They are not the nicest tasting mushrooms I have eaten;
their earthy taste and rubbery texture means that for this meal,
we need to force it down. They are, however, full of nutrients

that will help us sustain our energy until we are at least in a position to hunt for some proper food.

Whilst Laith catches up on some sleep, I remove the ancient spellbook from my satchel, the one that I have read from front to back hundreds of times over, along with some herbs and spices I have acquired on our travels. I try to read through the spellbook as frequently as I can to gain a better understanding of the words that are transcribed. My understanding of Elvish has improved dramatically with this book. Now I can read the hieroglyphs without the need of the scribbles in my notebook. After flicking through a few pages and reading over some of the protection spells, I combine turmeric, jarjoba fruit, and nutmeg with the last bit of water that I hold. As I drink it, the punchy taste explodes into my mouth. These ingredients combine well, and I know the remedy will help sustain my energy until we make a camp later today.

I watch over Laith while he sleeps. He carried himself well at the Redfearn house, though I know he is plagued by thoughts of his old master. I have watched him grow into a man these last few years. He is no longer the boy I took under my wing after Orjan abandoned him.

Reluctantly, I give him a light kick to the boot and watch him stir from his sleep.

"Come, Laith. I know you are tired, but we need to make further ground if we are to make camp."

Laith grumbles and mutters some words of discontent before leaning forward from the rock where he was perched.

"How long have I been asleep?" he asks, his eyes heavy and drawn. A light stubble has formed on his face.

"Long enough."

"We have marched down those hills for nearly two days, Jordell. My legs grow tired."

I smile to myself. In some ways, Laith is still a boy. I offer my bottle to him. Maybe some of this remedy will perk him up.

He shakes his head. "You drink it. Besides, I have age on my side, old man." He smirks at me and offers his hand. I grab hold of it and help heave him to his feet. As he straightens out his worn tunic, I drink the rest of the remedy and savour the taste. The sooner we find a running stream, the better, as even after drinking the remedy my throat still dries from thirst.

The greens of the higher, wetter hills are soon replaced by the dried yellow of harsh grasslands. It amazes me, the difference in the climate at the foot of the hills. There is little wildlife on these open plains, the lands getting harsher as we near the desert-like Biterian Plains. Small tufts of upturned grass leave circles of dried dirt, showing where moles have crept up to the surface. Every now and then I notice holes under the raised ground, a sign of rabbits.

"How much farther must we continue?" Laith asks.

"Have you learned nothing from me in all these years, Laith?"

"Shelter, cover, warmth," Laith answers monotonously, and I can't help but muster a laugh. "Shelter from the weather, cover from attacks, and warmth is a luxury."

"And do you see any of those things yet?" I ask.

He sighs. "No."

"Then I think we need to continue."

"How far away do you think this war is?" Laith kicks the stones on the ground as we walk.

"I fear it is closer than I would like."

"I will fight, Jordell. I am not afraid. The people of these lands need protecting, and I will fight for them." The compassion the boy shows is such a rare thing to come across in these times, and it saddens me to my core. He has always put the needs of others before his own.

"I know you will." I smile at him. "You need to understand that walking the path of always doing the right thing can often be the most difficult."

"I understand," he says, though I cannot help but think he is merely humouring me. "If we don't fight for these people, who will? I will protect people that need protecting for as long as they need me to. Whether they understand that or not. Is this not the right path to walk?"

"Unfortunately, Laith, that is not the world we live in, and others across Levanthria would not share your views. They would enforce hardships on others to maintain their coin and comfort. The reason I warn you is because it is easier for a good person to walk a dark path when they see the torment that the world can bring, than it is for a bad person to turn good. Take Ulrik, for example. I have no doubt that there is good in there. But they seem twisted by the anger that befalls them. Although they perceive themselves to have done a good deed in assassinating the king, is that itself not a dark path to walk? Where do you draw the line?"

"You talk in riddles old man. What about Vireo?" Laith counters. "He was a bad person when I first met him. Now he helps protect those in need and offers them shelter in the forest alongside him. Free from the hardships of living in Askela."

"True. Vireo has been able to redeem himself, but I am sure he will still have regrets and enemies from the life that he once lived. There is a difference between being a bad person and being an evil person. This is the line I warn about. I fear that once it is crossed, there is no number of good deeds that can redeem a person."

My attention is distracted from something in the distance, something peculiar that lies just ahead of us.

"What's that?" Laith asks.

I squint against the light of the sun. Whatever it is, it seems out of place on these barren fields.

"Is it a scarecrow?"

I shake my head. "These plains are too harsh for crops; it would be madness to try and grow anything here." I examine the surrounding landscape. "It's time to turn west before we end up having to walk Gondoron Pass. But I guess it will not harm us to have a look."

We continue towards the object in the distance until we are close enough to make out more of the shape.

"It's a person," Laith calls, shielding his gaze from the burning sun. Without hesitation, he sets off at speed towards the figure.

"Be careful boy, it could be a trap!" I scold as I start to run after him. The boy is rash in his decision-making and often acts before thinking. Something he will need to grow out of, for both of our sakes. My chest heaves as I wade through the spiked grass which scratches against my legs. Laith covers the ground faster than me and reaches the person first.

It is a woman, wearing clothes I am not familiar with, as if she is from the wild. Her torso and arms are on display, her skin etched with blue swirling symbols and designs. She is splattered with blood, yet I do not see any mortal wounds. It is not her own.

"Be careful, Laith."

"Here, help me get her down." Laith removes a dagger and hacks at the ropes that bind her hands. Her head lulls backwards, revealing a face burnt from the sun, her lips swelled and cracked from dehydration. Blood soaks her plaited auburn hair, and I see a gash on her crown where she has been struck.

Just who is this woman? And how did she come to be here? The only thing I am certain of is that whoever left her here intended for her to die a long and painful death.

5

LAITH

"Grab this." I show Jordell the rope I need him to keep hold of to stop the woman crashing to the ground. She is not in a good way, and I fear she may be close to death. Who would do this to a person?

Jordell grabs hold of the rope as I ask, and I move to the front of the post where the woman is tied. I would place her around my age, but it is hard to tell given her bruised and swollen face.

"Let go of the rope."

As Jordell releases, the woman stoops forward and I catch her.

"I've got you," I reassure her, although I am not sure if she can hear me. I lower her to the ground as delicately as I can. Reaching for my water, I tilt her head upright slightly and place the bottle against her cracked lips. The liquid splashes against her, and her mouth slowly moves as she takes what must be her first drink in days, if not longer.

"Who do you think has done this? Why would someone do this?" I ask. I find it deplorable that someone would be left in such a state. Whoever has done this holds no honour, and my blood boils with frustration at what they have done.

"She may have committed a crime."

"There is no Levanthrian law that dictate this as a punishment. This doesn't make sense."

"Is she breathing?"

"Barely," I answer as I watch her chest rise and fall ever so slightly.

Jordell drops to his knees and pours out the contents of his satchel, picking up different leaves and vials, sniffing and inspecting them. "I don't have anything that can help. The gods have picked today as her day."

"The gods will have to wait!" I bark. After everything that we have seen, after everything that we have been subjected to, it frustrates me that Jordell still turns to the wisdom of the gods. "Jordell, there must be something you can do."

Jordell stares at the woman blankly for a few moments before moving to her side. "I will do what I can." He mutters words under his breath, his eyes pinned shut whilst he concentrates. His hands glow with a burning white light that he has warned me in the past not to stare into, so I shield my eyes. He plants his hands onto the woman's abdomen, and she writhes and recoils, a pained noise escaping her lips. Jordell continues to utter his incantation as the ground around them pulsates, soft waves of vibrations emitting from them both. With each pulsing beat, the vibrations get stronger and harder. Sweat beads on Jordell's head and he grimaces as he concentrates his magic on the woman who continues to writhe around, squirming against the dirt where she lies.

"She is close to the afterlife. I have never tried this level of recovery before." Jordell continues to push his hands down against her with all his might as though he fights against an unknown force to maintain contact with her. He strains his arms and clenches his jaw whilst he draws on power like I have not seen from him before. The ground continues to shake and rumble as Jordell draws on further magic, the dirt skipping off the ground in a circle around them.

"Aaaaargh!" Jordell screams in pain. His arms buckle under the intense pressure, then the largest of pulses pushes out from around them. It is powerful enough to knock me from my feet, and I slam to the ground, intense pain shooting down my side where I land on small stones.

A cloud of dust surrounds Jordell and the strange woman. As it settles, Jordell sits back on the heels of his feet and plants his hands on his knees, gulping down the air around him. His clothes are laden with dust and his breath is laboured, the dirt sticking to his clammy face.

"Are you okay?" I rush to his side to steady him.

After a few more deep intakes of breath, he replies, "I have never drawn on that much magic before."

"Come, you need to rest." I am familiar with the afflictions that come with magic-use, which is why Jordell is so careful about using it. I know that he will suffer for what he has done, and I can only hope his efforts haven't gone to waste.

Jordell gives me a light nod to tell me he will be okay. "I just . . . I just need a moment to gather myself."

I spin on my knees next to the woman to check her over. She does not appear to be breathing. Dust settles on her sun-kissed face, giving her a paler complexion. "No, no, no. That can't have been for nothing." I curse.

The woman lets out a gasp of air as if she had been submerged underwater for a time. She laughs and splutters as she breathes in the dust that still floats in the air, then her eyes bolt open wide. I am instantly drawn to their emerald-green colour, marbled with blue like ice encased in the rarest of gemstones. Her gaze darts around, panic-stricken, unsure of what just happened. When her eyes meet mine, I give her a smile, but her face turns to worry. Her hand catches me in the midrib as she reaches for my knife. Before I have a chance to snatch her wrist, she removes the blade and rolls away from me.

"Woah, slow down. We just helped you," I tell her, but she frantically scrambles on her backside away from me until her back reaches a mound and she can move no farther. She points the dagger towards me, her hands shaking.

"*Draga regaro dregam*," she says in a tongue that I am unfamiliar with.

"Do you recognise that language?" I ask Jordell.

"I do not know what language she speaks. Be careful, Laith."

"Who did this to you?" I ask, knowing that she will not be able to answer my words.

"*Dregam!*" she repeats, jabbing the knife at me as a gesture of warning.

"I am not going to hurt you," I tell her. "My friend, he just healed you of your wounds. At great cost to himself."

The woman stares intently into my eyes, her jaw tight, her knuckles whitening round the dagger. Thinking for a moment about how I might placate her, I remove my belt that holds my sword. I keep it sheathed and raise it in front of me. "See, I mean no harm to you." Then I toss my weapon away from us towards Jordell. It bounces across the dirt until sliding to a stop, leaving me in an even more vulnerable position.

The woman is frenzied, her eyes darting between myself and Jordell, her blade firmly fixed on me. Then her eyes roll, and her arm drops to her side. As her hand opens, the blade spills to the ground and I realise she is fainting. I move quickly and slide onto my knees by her side, catching her before her head can hit the ground.

"Will she be okay?" I ask, looking up at Jordell.

"I certainly hope so, otherwise I am to endure the pain that is to come for no reason."

"Are *you* okay?" I ask.

"I am afraid I will need to make camp before we continue. I need to let the affliction run its course." Jordell's face drops with worry, his wrinkled face pained with the knowledge of what is about to come. "I can already feel the pain travelling through my arms as though made of fire whilst being submerged in the coldest water." He grimaces as he pulls his sleeves over his forearm. I see blackened skin before he covers it up.

"Come," I tell him, scooping the mysterious woman up in my arms. "I will keep watch over you both whilst you rest."

Jordell gets to his feet and gingerly follows, wincing with every step that he takes. After a short walk I spot some small mounds that will give us cover. The ground has already been worn underneath, creating a curved arch overhead. With any luck, I will be able to snare us something to eat during the night.

Jordell limps to our new camp and sits with his back to the mound. He does not reply, he simply breathes in and out and focuses his mind. In this moment I know that this will be the longest night he will have ever endured. The fact that he is willing to endure this pain to ease the suffering of another shows all I need to know of his character and the reason why I trust him more than anyone. Guilt consumes me for the fleeting moment that I considered leaving Jordell to search for Orjan. I banish the thoughts for now as I focus on supporting Jordell, to get through what is to come.

6

JORDELL

"*The Lords and Baroness' of the land are throwing their names into the reckoning for who will be the next ruler of Levanthria. The Great Temple insist that royal protocol must ensue meaning that there will be a month of mourning before a new King or Queen is selected. However not everyone agrees with following the Great Temple's royal protocol.*"

LETTER to the court of Byron, Coratios Vex, 255 KR

THE BLACKENED sky above grants me little comfort from the torment. Waves of pain wash over me, again and again, each crashing blow stabbing at my skin like daggers. My body fights it, but it is to no avail. This is a pain I must endure. Like the air that we breathe in and out, magic is a force that must run its course.

The stars above decorate the skies and I wonder which of the gods watch over me. Would they approve of my actions, or is this my punishment for using forbidden powers? Another wave crashes into me, causing my arms to burn, and I can't help but let out an agonised cry of pain. The burning is quickly followed by an ice-cold sensation coursing through my veins. It cools my arms for a brief moment before the chill takes over and a dull ache sets in. Then the burning feeling returns. Each time the pain seeps back in, I writhe around in torment, my dignity long forgotten, my screams loud enough to scare away any predators of the night.

Laith sits by the fire, his gaze fixed on the mysterious woman.

Since I met Laith, I have not known him to spend any time with a woman other than Gillam. He is studying her the way I study my spellbook: a mystery to be deciphered.

The fire burns, not too brightly but just enough to keep the other two warm. I lie as far away from it as possible, unable to stand the heat generated by the flames against my corrupted skin.

My body jolts and spasms uncontrollably, and a sharp pain stabs at my stomach as I curl up into a ball like a helpless babe just born from the womb. I then straighten as I feel a seizure coming along, and I have no control over my body as I convulse.

"Jordell!" Laith moves to my side and tries to hold me steady. I wish to thank him but no words leave my mouth. Just a jumbled gargle that neither of us can make out. I am a prisoner of my own mind, able to see everything that is going on around me but unable to influence it. Every stab, every burn, every pain unbearable as if I am in some hellscape created for only those who have committed the worst sins.

When my convulsions finally stop, a nauseating feeling comes over me. The heat of bile rises within as if I might breathe fire.

Recognising the signs, Laith heaves me onto my side, his hands like red-hot pokers as he plants them on my back. I let out a howl of pain, and Laith pulls my long white hair back as I retch uncontrollably until the limited contents of my stomach greet me once more.

"Here, have some water." He places his bottle against my lips and tips it up. I try to pull my head away but the water washes into my mouth. I swallow some before gargling and spluttering. It feels as though I have just drunk molten rock. This is the worst my affliction has ever been, and I do not know how much longer I can endure such pain.

The woman stirs by the fire, recovering from her own form of torture. I feel a sense of regret over my actions, over the fact I lie here in this excruciating pain, all because I chose to help a complete stranger. Shame overcomes me at my darkened thoughts.

All I can do is let this affliction run its course. It is the burden I must bear for the power I have drawn upon, the cost I must pay for saving another's life.

7

LAITH

The sky begins to turn dark purple as the dawn greets us. I am exhausted and in dire need of sleep, but I must stand watch over these two. Jordell rocks slowly back and forth, staring at the ground. He has not said a word since he stopped writhing around on the floor, the haunting echoes of his screams ringing out across these plains.

Jordell has become the father figure that I never had. He has taught me so much on our travels, and I owe a great debt to him. If I could swap places with him, I would.

"You need to rest," Jordell tells me, his voice hoarse as if he has swallowed glass. "You haven't slept." He speaks as though uttering his words is an arduous task.

"But you —"

"I will be fine when day breaks," he cuts me off, his eyes still unmoving. "You need to rest if we are to continue our journey. You will be no use to anyone if exhaustion creeps in."

"Very well, wake me if she begins to stir."

The woman breathes lightly by the fire, wrapped in my cloak. I lie back by the fire and stare up at the stars, wondering at first if I will be able to fall asleep. My body is devoid of energy, however, and as my mind searches for the answers in the stars I find my consciousness drifting away with the passing clouds.

I am woken by the smell of cooked meat and the pangs of hunger cause my stomach to growl louder than I have ever heard it. I breathe in the fragrant smell once more. It isn't just meat, it is thyme and garlic, too. When I open my eyes, the light above causes me to squint. Day has well and truly broken, and in a panic I sit bolt upright to survey my surroundings. The woman still lies unconscious on the other side of the fire. Jordell kneels next to me, his face weary and gaunt, though he is clearly over the worst of his affliction. He is tending to the meat skewed onto a makeshift spit that he must have fashioned whilst I slept.

"I am pleased to say your snares did their job," Jordell says, smiling as he rotates the rabbit that cooks on the fire. I notice two other rabbits lying by his satchel with his ingredients.

"Are you feeling better?" I ask. "I've never seen anybody struggle with pain like that before."

"My head simply throbs now as though I sank plenty of ale last night." He musters a laugh which turns into a cough partway through.

I move to aid him, but Jordell waves me away as he removes the rabbit from the spit. Its juices drip into the open fire, causing the flames to lick the meat as Jordell places it down on a rock beside him. He blows on it whilst eyeing it like a ravenous beast himself. It has been days since we ate anything substantial.

"You first," I say, "you need to get your energy back up after yesterday."

"Thank you." He rips one of the legs off and bites into the fatty part of the rabbit's thigh, the juices running down his beard. He chews through the meat in no time before ripping more from the rabbit's side.

I cannot begin to think of the ordeal Jordell has been through. There is no harder thing than seeing someone you care about endure such pain and being powerless to do anything to help.

As another wave of hunger threatens to rip open my stomach, Jordell raises his ravenous eyes and his momentary wildness evaporates like a passing storm.

"Etiquette seems to have forsaken me, I do apologise." He casts me a smile but looks embarrassed to have eaten as though he were a man of the wild. In truth, we *are* men of the wild. We have held no home or base since leaving Vireo in the Forest of Opiya. It is something that I would like for us to have one day, a place to live, somewhere to stay. Somewhere where we don't have to be looking over our bastard shoulders every second of every day. What I would give for that life.

Reaching for the rabbit, I tear off some meat from the side. It is greasy to the touch but I enjoy every second of stuffing the contents into my mouth, savouring every bite.

A murmur to my side draws my attention back to the mysterious woman. Just who is she? I have so many questions to ask her but if she does not speak our tongue, I do not know how I will broach such subjects.

I leave Jordell to our feast and move to the woman's side. Her eyes remain closed as if in peaceful sleep, but her face is bruised, her body bloodied. The painted art covering her arms and body fascinate me. Swirls of blue, not necessarily denoting any pictures in particular but forming flowing colour over her like tribal waves. The paint traces over her stomach and my gaze lingers longer on her bare skin than it should, her toned muscles covered with what looks to be an emblem of a sun around the centre.

When I look at her peaceful face again, my heart skips as I realise her eyes are wide open and she stares into my own as if examining my soul. She kicks out, knocking me away from her as she scrambles backwards away from me.

"No, no, no, I didn't mean – I wasn't –" words stumble from my mouth as though I am an infant who can only babble. I take in a deep breath and compose myself. "I am not going to hurt you. I wouldn't do anything like that to you or anyone."

The woman's eyes dart from me to Jordell but then remain in Jordell's direction. It doesn't take a genius to realise that the woman is likely more starving than we are. Only the gods know how long she was tied up to that post.

"Here, have this." I walk to the fire and tear the rabbit's remaining hind leg from its carcass, then kneel in front of the woman. I offer her the food slowly, leaving my outstretched hand hanging in the air. She stares at me, hesitant.

"Take it." I smile in an attempt to reassure her. "It is not poisoned, we want to help you."

An awkward moment passes between us where I remain knelt with my arm outstretched. If there was a ring in my hand one would be forgiven for believing I was proposing.

The woman rushes forward and snatches the meat from my hand, then starts gnawing at it, her focus solely on her meal. It only takes a few moments before she has finished, and she looks at me again before her eyes shift to the cooked rabbit.

"You want some more." I smile again. At least the woman is no longer striking me with every opportunity she is presented with. I grab the rabbit and tear a larch chunk of meat from its side, making sure some remains for myself. "Here, have some more, it isn't much, but it will be enough to help get you back on your feet."

The woman's brow frowns as if she is not sure she should trust me. I would not blame her for thinking this way. After all, we have only just met. She takes the rabbit from me and starts tucking into it.

Placing my hand to my chest, I take the opportunity to try and break through to her. "My name is Laith." I point at Jordell who shuffles around packing up his satchel. "This is Jordell."

The woman sits pondering on my words. She does not speak our tongue, so perhaps I am foolish to try and explain our names.

Then the woman raises a weakened arm and places her closed fist against her chest. "Yaelor," she says.

8

JORDELL

" *I have a plan, one of which I have been laying the foundations for years. The final piece of the puzzle lies to the north east of Levanthria in the form of a dwarf who I have been informed has invented something most curious. A powder which is said to hold the power of the gods.* "

SECRET DIARY OF TARIN VIERGHOST, 254 KR

MY BODY ACHES as though I have been trampled by a hundred horses. Each time I move, my body snaps as my stiffened joints bring me back to reality with a painful crack. Last night was torturous. It is a night that I never wish to relive.

Occasional shivers and waves of warmth pulsate through my body, causing me to feel as though thousands of small needles pierce my skin at any given moment. Compared to last night, this pain is minimal.

As I come around from my magic-use, the temptation to

use one of my healing spells on myself is only comparable to the addiction of one who consumes too much ale. It takes every ounce of my will not to succumb to the temptation to ease the pain in my body. My arms are the worst, and as I reach for my satchel, I notice a blackened wound on the back of my hand. The skin is cracked with small, dark veins extending out from it. I touch it with my free hand and wince at the pain. It is tender to the touch, and the skin feels broken and dried.

I take out my worn leather-bound journal from my satchel and make a quick entry about healing the mysterious woman as best as I can, though I struggle to hold my quill and my hand tremors uncontrollably. I need to gather my thoughts in this moment, to truly capture how I am feeling. I have found that my memory tends to forget the pain and torment I endure when succumbing to the aftereffects of magic-use. It is as though my mind shrouds these memories, making the temptation to cast spells for menial tasks all too appealing once again.

I finish my scribbles and blow on the ink before returning my journal to my satchel.

"Are you able to walk?" Laith asks.

"I am not that old that I am crippled." My shortness seems to surprise Laith, and I sigh. "Sorry, I did not mean to snap."

"It's okay." Laith offers me a hand which I gratefully accept, and he heaves me to my feet, my body snapping and cracking like broken branches. The ache is bad but bearable. I shuffle to Yaelor who remains sitting by a large stone. Her eyes are vacant as if her thoughts are somewhere else.

"Do you speak our tongue?" I ask her.

My words startle her and bring her back into our presence. She quickly looks around camp as if surveying an exit route, then seems to remember where she is.

Yaelor gives me a slight nod. "I do." Her accent is not from these lands, but her words are clear and unbroken.

"I have something for you." I reveal a remedy that remains parcelled in a leaf. After all, I was an apothecary before I became a mage. "This will help prevent your wounds from becoming infected." I open up the leaf to reveal a dark green paste inside. The earth notes from the mushrooms and choya seeds that I have ground together are an acquired taste, but one I have become familiar with from my days of tending people at the Great Temple in Askela.

Yaelor is hesitant and I do not blame her. The setting feels calm, a gentle breeze in the air and birds cawing from the nearby trees and rocks where they perch, waiting for any scraps of food we may offer. Laith is busy tending to the fire, his back to us.

"Watch." I place the parcel on the ground and turn over my hand, revealing the small black wound. I wipe my finger in the thick paste, then smear it over the wound on the back of my hand. A bolt of sharp pain shoots up my arm and down my fingers.

"What caused that?" Yaelor asks. I am surprised at how fluent she is in our language.

"Magic," I answer. "Magic I used to heal you. Unfortunately, using any kind of magic in this world has its consequences, it comes at a price."

"Will it heal?" Her voice is soft but assertive.

"Only time will tell." I smile, trying my hardest to allay my own fears for what this wound means. I rub the paste until it covers the wound on my hand in full, trying to ignore the burning sensation.

"Will you allow me?" I ask.

"If you must."

I kneel next to her, my knees cracking in the process. I take the paste and rub it on the cut above her swollen eye. She doesn't so much as wince. I rub the paste into her arms, then offer it to her to rub onto the cuts on her legs and torso.

"The smell will take a little getting used to, but those wounds should be fine in no time. I would need to keep an eye on you for the coming days if you would not mind. Just to make sure no infection takes you. You are free to leave at any time, including when your wounds have healed," I explain. I have endured too much to allow Yaelor to fall victim to a nasty infection.

"I have nowhere else to go." Yaelor looks away from me as if searching for something across the Biterian Plains.

"What happened to you?" Laith asks, "If you don't mind me asking. It isn't everyday you stumble across someone tied up, beaten, and left for the birds."

"I have lost everything. My father, my tribe, my honour." Yaelor looks down at the ground, downcast. As though a darkened shadow creeps over her as she talks. "We came to an agreement, one through which my father hoped to gain land to build a new life for our people. Lord Breyton offered us that land if we came to help him in Eltera. My father was the chieftain of our tribe. He agreed to the terms and brought our people across the seas to help Lord Breyton take Eltera. Everything went to plan until a spellcaster stormed our camp at night and killed my father."

Yaelor seems conflicted as she fights with her memories, her face torn with the pain of reliving her past. "In this moment my people looked at me as chieftain and despite some of them wishing to return to our land, I insisted that we storm Eltera. I wanted revenge for my father's death, and to fulfil the deal made with Breyton."

"You tried to storm Eltera?" Laith responds. "What happened?"

"We were told that the kingdom was ready for taking, they

just needed our numbers to squash the last of a resistance. We were not prepared for an ambush. We were not prepared to fight against monsters."

"Monsters?" I ask.

"A monster led their defences, he held a line against us. He was not like anything I have seen before. His skin was scaled, his eyes as yellow as the tunic he wore, his mouth filled with sharp teeth. He was more lizard-like than man."

"A lizard-man?" I ask, casting an eye at Laith. Why would Orjan fight alongside Morgana? It doesn't seem that Laith has picked up on this link yet, though, so I allow the conversation to continue without interruption.

"He was not alone, he fought alongside the powerful spell-caster who slayed my father, her green magic like nothing I have ever seen before. They fought with fury and without hesitation, they slaughtered anyone on the battlefield that was against them. One by one, Breyton's soldiers fell, men and women alike. I could see that we were losing our own warriors at an alarming pace. In this moment I showed weakness against my enemy whilst fighting against the spellcaster." Yaelor's expression becomes stony, and she pauses, fighting back tears.

In this moment I have no doubt that it is Morgana who she speaks of. She is the only person I have come across whose necromancy power is of this colour, the only one who has mastered the truly forbidden magic.

"I ordered our warriors to retreat before it was too late. Magic is not natural, but even the spells she cast were far darker than I ever expected."

"So how did you come to end up tied up to a post?" Laith asks.

"The Barbaraqs see retreat as an act of cowardice. The elders within my tribe made their rage known. This is why you found me in that state, dishonoured and exiled by my own people. I am left with nothing. It is a fate that I deserve."

"No, you don't," Laith scolds her. "You saved the lives of your people. Jordell, do you think the spellcaster was Morgana?"

"You speak her name?" Yaelor's eyes widen, her curiosity piqued.

"We have crossed paths before," I tell her. "She is a dark sorceress, and draws on a truly forbidden magical force, one which consumes the life force of her enemies." She is the only sorceress I know who is able to transfer wounds from one person to another.

"She drew her magic from others, is this something you do?"

"No," I answer sternly. "The power she wields is one that no one should possess. Any magic I use draws on my own life source. It is why you see me in such a frail state."

"What of the lizard-man?" Laith cuts in, and I know in an instant where Laith's thoughts delve.

"He wore the colours of a kingdom that occupies our lands, across the seas. His torn tunic bore the crest of Rashouya, and his weapon was like nothing I have seen before. A spiked metal ball at the end of his sword."

Laith pales. "It is Orjan, it must be Orjan," he says with conviction, finally connecting the pieces of the puzzle. "But that doesn't make any sense. Jordell, why would he fight alongside her? Orjan wouldn't do that, not unless he was being made to." Laith now echoes the same questions that run through my own mind.

"You speak as though you know of this monster." Yaelor cuts Laith a look of confusion.

Is this a sign from the gods that our paths have crossed, that this information has found its way to us?

"I need to go, we need to go to Eltera. I need to know if it is him." Laith paces back and forth.

"We need to stay our true path, of which we are already delayed," I remind him. "Laith, you cannot go. To do so would be madness. We are wanted men, and we have a Barbaraq with us who recently attacked them. It would be suicide to wander in as we are."

"I understand this, Jordell, but what else am I to do? It has been years since I saw him last. He was the first person to teach me how to fight, to teach me what it means to have honour. I cannot agree that he has taken to fighting alongside our enemy, I cannot believe that he has fallen so far. I must see him, it is the only way I can be sure."

I have never seen Laith this heightened before. "You have my word that we will look to find out more, but for now we must continue to the Forest of Opiya." I walk towards him and rest my hands on his shoulders, forcing him to look into my eyes.

"We will find out, Laith, I promise you. But we *must* find the Elder Tree. We seek answers that are bigger than Orjan, bigger than you and me."

Laith nods in understanding, but something flickers in his eyes. Something I'm not sure I can trust.

9

LAITH

Luscious, soft green grass replaces the dried yellow spikiness of the plains as we set off across the northern territory of Eltera, avoiding the treacherous Gondoron Pass. My legs are tired but we need to continue on our journey if we are to make good progress. How Jordell remains at his pace even after recovering from his magic-use amazes me.

Yaelor wears my cloak which provides her with some modesty from the bare skin on display from her Barbaraq clothing. She has not complained once of the walk so far, but has simply got on with it, following behind Jordell. I can see from her limp that she struggles with the pain, but through rugged determination she continues as if it does not ail her.

Thoughts of Orjan preoccupy my mind. Orjan fights alongside Morgana, but why? The day he cast me away, I always understood; he was broken and humiliated. He tried to get his life back on track, but the consequences of his drunken decisions caught up with him one too many times.

I was his squire for two years. He fed me, looked after me,

trained me. I had known him, I had seen the honour he sought to regain. I can't accept the information that Yaelor has passed, let alone understand how he comes to bear the appearance of a lizard-man.

I know it would be insanity to head to Eltera, but the temptation to see Orjan is great. I want answers. I want to understand how, after the two years we had, he cast me aside as if I did not matter. He was my sire, and I would have stayed with him, I would have helped him.

Yaelor lifts her head high and halts suddenly. I stop behind her as she kneels to inspect the dew-sodden grass.

"Horses," she says. "These tracks look fresh."

"Is everything okay?" Jordell huffs as he stops, regaining his breath.

"Yaelor has found horse tracks," I answer. It has been an age since we last had a horse, and the thought of riding one makes my feet ache all the more. To be able to travel and not have to walk the journey would be truly amazing.

"A luxury," I say wistfully.

Jordell glowers at me. "A luxury long forgotten."

"I swear on my life, Jordell, those horses were tied up!"

"Yet we find ourselves horseless and on foot all this time." His sarcasm irks me, but he has every reason to be frustrated with me for losing the horses that we did have.

"We will not be horseless for long," Yaelor muses. "Over there."

Yaelor draws our attention to further across the open field where a group of horses grazes peacefully, enjoying the sun as it creeps into life.

"They are wild horses, Yaelor. We can't just walk over and hop on," I point out.

"You can't?" She is visibly puzzled by my statement. Without a moment's hesitation, she unclips my cloak and lets it drop to the ground. My eyes fix on her bare skin, her modesty only just covered by the trail of Barbaraq clothing. "Stay here, this journey will take too long on foot, and we will heal better if we travel on horse."

Without any other warning, Yaelor crouches down and walks towards the horses as they graze.

"What are we to do?" I ask Jordell.

"Given you are about as subtle as a stone dropping into a lake, I would suggest you stay there as you have been told. Those horses would be onto you in a moment and likely bolt."

He has a point. Stealth is not a strong point of mine.

The way Yaelor walks is predatory as she makes her way to the horses. Somehow, she remains hidden and the horses do not startle. She brings her hands to her mouth and makes a strange clicking sound, almost birdlike. The horses raise their heads and start to walk slowly in her direction.

"How in the blazes did she do that?"

"I have no idea, boy, but I am most certainly impressed."

She crouches down in the longer grass and waits patiently as the herd of horses pass her path. I find myself holding my breath as I watch in anticipation. Then when the opportunity strikes, she leaps up from the grass and pounces on a grey mare at the back of the group. She grabs hold of its mane as it sets off at a gallop, and I fear it is going to drag her through the grass. To my surprise, she quickly pulls herself up onto the back of the horse with startling agility, firmly planting her hands in its mane.

"How on earth did she do that?" I wonder aloud, not searching for a response but merely in awe of what I have just witnessed. The horse bucks as it attempts to dismount her, but she sits firmly, pulling herself closer to the horse's back. It tilts its head up and she pulls away before kicking her heels into the horse's side. It bucks again but she remains unmoved, her determination shining through. She perseveres and remains seated on the horse. I think she's finished, but then she starts chasing the remaining horses in the herd.

She rides the grey mare as if she has known it far longer, a feat that I find amazing. To my shock, she rallies the rest of the horses in our direction.

"Is she doing what I think she is?" I ask as the herd stampedes in our direction.

"I do believe she is." Jordell cracks his neck as though limbering up.

"There's no way I can do what she has just done! This is madness," I cry out, flailing my arms out in disbelief at what we are about to attempt.

"Well, with that attitude you are likely not going to achieve anything." Jordell plants his feet and hitches up his tunic to enable him more mobility.

I feel the ground shake as the horses draw close. Yaelor's face is wide with joy. As the horses draw closer, my heart thunders harder than their hooves hitting the ground. I reach out wildly as a brown horse with a black mane passes in front of me. My shoulder is nearly pulled from its socket as I grasp the horse's rough mane. The pain is jarring, and I cry out as my head snaps back, causing the world around me to blur. Somehow, I keep hold, but as I take a few steps I start to lose my footing due to the speed we are running. Then I make an attempt to swing up on top of the horse.

I fail miserably. My body bounces off the side of the horse and my legs trail behind me through the grass as I cling on in desperation. My shoulder sears wildly as though it is on fire, and my grip loosens. I know I have little time to try and heave myself on top.

It is as though the horse reads my mind. As I try and force myself on its back, the animal starts to buck. Its hind legs hit me in the side like a battering ram and I cannot hold on any longer. I crash into the ground, bouncing off the turf like a stone skimming across water. I roll to a stop and let out a groan of pain, my body aching everywhere. Raising my head, I see horses galloping off into the distance, my chance of obtaining one long passed. I let my head drop into the grass and stare up at the vibrant blue sky that is decorated with shrouds of white clouds. I am frustrated with myself, at the missed opportunity. My heart races and my body hurts and it was all for nothing. As the throbbing in my head starts to subside, I notice the laughter.

"What on earth was that, Laith?" Jordell chuckles wildly, clearly impressed at whatever it was that he just saw me do.

As I stare up into the sky, two horse heads come into place, obscuring my view. "How the bloody hell did you get up there?" I ask as I sit myself up. I am aghast at seeing Jordell sitting smugly atop a black horse. He is gathering his breath, but somehow he has managed to mount it.

"It has been many years since I did anything like that." He smiles. "You see, it is all about the timing, Laith." His horse bucks slightly but Jordell manages to settle it.

Yaelor sits on top of her grey steed, a smile brimming from one side of her face to the other. "He is inexperienced at riding?" she asks Jordell as if I am not present, and I feel my cheeks redden.

"Thanks to Yaelor, we will be able to travel more efficiently," Jordell explains, leaning forward to pat his horse on the side of its neck.

"You ride with me," Yaelor proclaims, and she shuffles back on her horse. "You do know how to ride, don't you?" I do not know if she teases me or is genuinely worried that I do not know how to ride a horse.

"I know how to ride a horse!" I fire back, embarrassed by

the whole situation. In truth I have never felt more pressure than in this moment to successfully mount a horse. I ready myself and jump up, grabbling hold of the horse's mane and swinging my leg over the top. Yaelor leans back to avoid my leg knocking her off, but despite the pressure I put myself under, I have made it onto the horse's back.

"See, that wasn't too difficult," Yaelor teases as she shuffles in behind me. Her breath catches the back of my neck and I feel the hairs on my neck and arms rise. I have never ridden with a woman before. Come to which I have never ridden a horse bareback before, let alone a wild one. Jordell grins at the awkward situation I find myself in and at how uncomfortable I must look.

"You know what to do, right?" Yaelor asks rather expectantly.

"I've never done this before," I confess. "I've ridden horses before, just never like this."

"Oh," Yaelor says, "okay." She leans right into my back, and I feel her body press against my own. "Lean forward!" she scolds.

I awkwardly do as I am told, and her arms wrap around me as she takes a tight grip of the horse's mane. I do the same and my hands sit just inside her own.

"Come, we will cover ground far faster now," Jordell exclaims. "Well done, Yaelor. You have proven yourself most useful. Thank you. The sooner we can find some cover to travel in the better, it is not wise to stay out in the open given we are all wanted by the Crown, or whoever it is that is running the kingdom in the absence of the king's death."

Jordell kicks his heels into the back of his horse and sets off at pace.

Yaelor does the same and we follow. My worries of falling off the horse are allayed as Yaelor pins me into place. I can't help but feel embarrassed about my inexperience, but grateful that she controls the horse that we ride.

The ground passes quickly as we make our way across the field. After a time I notice some trees ahead.

"Is that the Forest of Opiya?" I ask.

"No, it's some old woodlands that sit between the forest and Eltera," Jordell answers. I am in awe at just how well he knows these lands. "It will provide some much-needed cover as we progress and hopefully I will be able to grab some ingredients too."

I agree with Jordell; these fields are far too open. It would be wiser for us to travel in cover. Our chances of survival feel greater now that there are three of us in our party.

With the comfort of Yaelor behind me, my worries about Orjan fade away.

10

JORDELL

Two days of travel puts us deeper into the woodlands. The canopy of trees above allows light to sparkle across the ground. The colours around us are beautiful, the vibrant needles of the pine trees evergreen, unlike the yellow and brown leaves that have begun to fall from the other trees. They scatter around the ground underneath us like a broken jigsaw, misplaced but somehow still managing to connect along the trail that we lead. The smell of the leaves is calming, a combination of wood, sap, and earth grounding me in this moment. The chirping of birds rings out amongst the trees as we pass through. Having never travelled through these woods, I am unsure of what creatures inhabit these lands.

I do not feel on edge as we travel through these parts for some reason. Maybe it is the trees, maybe it is the shelter. I feel rested following my magic-use, but my hand does draw a level of concern from me. The throbbing sensation grows stronger, the paste I applied doing little to stem whatever kind of wound it is. I look at my hand and notice that the gash grows bigger, the blackened veins tracking up my arm. You would be forgiven for mistaking them for tree roots, such is the way they twist and turn up my forearm.

Laith sits upright on his horse, holding the mane confidently. Yaelor continues to sit behind him with her hands planted on the tops of her thighs.

"I find these trees amazing," Yaelor says, her eyes agape in wonderment at what surrounds us. "In my lands we are surrounded by sands. Such a sight is a beauty to behold."

I don't reply or acknowledge Yaelor's words, distracted within my own thoughts.

"What is it?" Laith asks.

I try to pull my sleeve back down my arm, not wanting to cause any unnecessary worry.

"Let me see your hand," Laith demands. There is no getting by him, the boy does not miss a trick.

"It's okay, Laith. I am sure if we can find some ingredients, I will be able to create some more paste to help it heal. Do not concern yourself."

"Let me see it," Laith demands sternly, his eyes fixed on my arm.

I reluctantly raise my sleeve to reveal the blackened wound and dark veins protruding from my arms.

"By the gods!" Laith proclaims. "Jordell, what is happening to your arm? Why did you not tell me?" His face is a picture of worry and I do not blame him; I worry myself.

"I fear my body breaks under the strain of the spells that I cast," I explain. "When we reach Vireo's settlement, I will have time to forage and read through the spellbook for answers." It is all I can hope that the luscious mushrooms and vegetables that grow in that enchanted place might contain magical properties that could help me heal. After all, the Forest of Opiya is home to many mysteries.

"Let's hope so, that looks awful."

I look at the tracked veins searching up my forearm, surprised at the speed they have spread these past days. I fear I may well need Laith to remove the arm if it gets worse; surely the tracking cannot continue if there is nothing attached to it. I keep this to myself, not wanting to concern Laith further.

All I know is that we must reach the Forest of Opiya as quickly as possible.

"Shh," Yaelor shushes us as she pulls on the back of Laith. "Stop."

Laith does as he is asked, and I follow suit, wondering what it is that has caught Yaelor's attention. She turns her head to the side as if listening more intently, her fraying red hair bound tightly to the back of her head.

"Something is ahead of us. Can you hear that?"

I lean forward and listen, hoping to draw on the quietness. Yaelor is correct. I can hear conversation between a group of people ahead of us. We only have two options: turn around, or continue our current path; there are no side roads for us to take.

"Hopefully it will be locals out chopping for wood," I say.

"And what if it isn't?" Laith asks.

"We have little option unless we travel back over our tracks."

Laith sighs, but nods.

I gee my horse on and lead the way, the voices growing louder. I find myself searching above the trees, hoping that the gods heed my prayers and let this be a harmless group.

My prayers go unanswered. Through the trees I see the black and gold colours of Askelan guards. Just what would they be doing out here, though?

"Did you find any?" a hoarse voice calls to the others.

"Not today," a scrawny guard answers.

"Fucking faeries. Stop sitting around and get searching! Codrin will not be impressed if we arrive empty-handed."

I motion to Yaelor and Laith to remain silent and turn around, but my horse huffs loudly, drawing unwanted attention to us in an instant.

"Fuck!" I curse loudly, which is most unlike me. "Follow my lead."

"Who goes there?" the hoarse voice calls out to us.

"Maybe it's the faeries," a woman sniggers.

"It sounds too big for a fucking faerie."

As we come into view, I survey the area and count five guards of varying size and no doubt experience. Three men and two women. Their camp is messy, with trees visibly hacked at and even a couple have been felled. One large tree balances against another, the base of it chopped away revealing a hollow inside.

Clearing my throat, I tell them, "We mean no harm, we are just passing through."

"Who are you?" the leader of the guards asks, his hand gripping the hilt of his blade. He is a stocky man, his black hair slicked back and his face ruffled with a greying beard.

"We have travelled from afar to forage in these woodlands. We do not seek any trouble." There is some truth in my words, but it remains to be seen if the guards will buy my story.

"I travel through these woodlands with my son and his new wife," I continue. "As you can see, my years are catching up with me. I bring my son here to show him where to find the terutian mushrooms. They fetch a good amount of coin amongst the sailors who we trade with. You see, these mushrooms help with sickness that overcomes those who travel by sea."

A stocky woman snaps her head back, her attention solely on us. "What did you hear us talking about?" she asks. She holds a woodcutter's axe in her hands. No doubt the trees have her to thank for their vandalism.

"Nothing that didn't sound like you are foraging here yourself. Are you in fact looking for terutian mushrooms as well? The secret is to search in the shadows of the rocks." My aim is to distract them enough so we can be on our way before they realise who we are.

I see the woman glance around, undoubtedly surveying for shadows beneath the rocks.

"Where is it you have travelled from?" the leader of the group asks, but his tone has shifted from interrogation to curiosity.

"Osar –"

"Uster," Laith answers at the same time.

I turn to face him and give a look that tells him in an instant that if I could curse him in this moment, I would. He looks away from me sheepishly. What was the fool thinking?

"I live in Osar, my son and his wife have recently taken a home in Uster."

"Is that true?" the woman calls, her shrill voice grating down my spine. I can tell she is well-trained and spoiling for a fight by her body language. "Uster was recently ransacked by the invading Barbaraqs. I heard there was nothing left but smouldering ruins."

"Exactly the right time to acquire land and property," I fire back. "Now, if it is okay, I would like to bid you a safe journey and continue on our task."

The woman lowers her axe. I nod my head and smile, urging my horse to continue on our path. My heart skips as the guards start to move out of our way. The gods appear to have offered us a kindness today.

"Wait a moment." The lead guard moves over to inspect us

further. He passes the front of my horse and makes his way to Laith and Yaelor behind me.

"When did you marry?" he asks Laith.

"Three weeks ago," he answers swiftly.

"Hmm." The guard muses as his eyes search over Yaelor who is thankfully covered by Laith's cloak.

"Very well, off you go. I would suggest leaving these woodlands if I was you, however."

"Thank you, sir," I answer, putting my hands together and bowing my head.

I jerk my head to the side hoping that Laith catches my cue. He does, and sets off with his horse to pass me. As he goes by, a gentle breeze lifts the side of the cloak Yaelor wears, revealing part of her paint-covered leg.

"Hang on!" The guard snatches up the hem of the cloak, revealing more of the blue markings on her skin.

"That is Barbaraq warpaint!" Without hesitation, he removes his blade and the other guards follow suit. The leader's eyes dart to me and then to Laith. "I know you! There is a price of coin on both your heads. You're the spellcaster!"

"I prefer the term wizard!"

It appears the gods have other plans for us after all.

II

LAITH

The Great Temple give their blessing to Lord Myrion Sand. He is the strongest candidate, has proved himself a master tactician on the battlefield and holds all the credentials that a King should possess, to lead our once glorious lands through the next age.

AYMARA BLYTHE, *Grand Priestess to the Great Temple, 255 KR*

"SHIT!" I quickly drive my boot into the face of the guard who has ousted us. I dismount my horse as quickly as I can, removing my sword from my side. One of the guards is upon me straight away and takes a wild swipe with his blade. I parry this before driving my blade across his stomach. As blood sprays across me, I grab hold of his hand and ram it down my blade, severing it at the wrist. His scream stops before he hits the leaf-covered ground. I toss the weapon to Yaelor who

61

quickly removes the mangled hand from the blade as she drops from the horse, ready to fight.

Two more guards approach and I begin duelling with them, hacking and swiping at one another, blocking attacks and attempting to strike them down. The female soldier with the axe charges at me, her eyes bulging with anticipation. She brings her weapon down towards me, but she is suddenly kneed sideways as Yaelor crashes into her.

My focus returns to the two guards in front of me. One of them strikes me in the face with his free hand before swinging his sword. I jump back, barely avoiding the swing before thrusting my sword forward. It pierces his stomach, and his mouth opens with shock. The remaining guard swings his sword and threatens to take my head clean off. I duck below it, and his blade instead removes the other guard's head. I dive towards him and tackle the man to the floor, striking his face twice before he rolls me from on top of him. He clutches his waist and retrieves a dagger which he holds with the blade pointing downwards. I adopt a defensive stance and raise my hands to fight him. He lunges, but I slap his dagger hand away and do the same when his other fist follows. When the third swing comes, I grab hold of his hand, bending it inwards until he impales himself with his own blade. His eyes widen as blood pools in his mouth, and he slumps to the earth.

To my right, Yaelor grapples with the guard bearing the axe. The two trade blows fiercely but Yaelor is skilled with the sword and forces the axewoman's weapon to the side before plunging her blade through her chest.

Only the leader remains. I see movement behind a large tree where Jordell is in combat himself. He moves well with his blade for someone of his age, and I recognize the steps he has spent the last few years teaching me. He knocks the guard back who stands defensively, his odds of survival minimal now that he is on his own against the three of us.

"You will pay for your insolence," he snarls, spit leaving his mouth, his slicked-back hair dropping in front of his face.

"This does not need to end with your death," Jordell says. "Lay down your weapon and leave, we will not attack you."

"Are you sure of this, Jordell?" I ask.

"We are not murderers. Your guards are dead because they attacked us. We will not continue this fight unless you instigate it."

"Scum, you're all scum," the guard hisses. He drops his sword to the ground, but he does not turn to leave. Instead, he reaches into his pocket and takes out a small vial of something. He grabs the cork with his teeth and pulls it out, then downs the contents in one.

"A coward's death," Yaelor spits.

"Either way, the man is unarmed," Jordell states.

The man drops to his knees and screams out in pain, his arms threatening to buckle from underneath him. The most he can hope for is that the poison grants him a swift death. It doesn't. He continues to writhe and grimace in pain for a few more moments before raising his head to greet us. The whites of his eyes have been replaced with a blackness only matched by the darkest of nights.

"You will pay, scum!"

"His hands!" I warn as I notice a glow emitting from them. The guard fires a blast of energy towards me, but he is wild with his aim and it flies past us, stripping the bark off a tree. Within seconds, he fires another blast, then another.

"Take cover!" Jordell bellows.

I head for the trees, blasts of energy shredding the ground around us as the guard displays his newfound magical abilities. As I hide behind a tree, my head throbs in tandem with my heartbeat, a loud ringing in my ears consuming my thoughts. The ground sprays up around us. My mind is dragged back to the Forest of Opiya, the first time I came across a spellcaster when we were ambushed, when I was captured and then whipped in front of everyone. It brings a panic about me, and I find my breathing quickening. To my horror, I am frozen to the spot, entombed in fear.

A blast of energy takes out a huge section of the tree that I hide behind and the force sends me crashing to the ground. The tree groans loudly, then begins to fall.

"Yaelor, look out!"

The falling tree moves towards her, but she hears my call and manages to dive out of the way as the trunk of the tree barely misses her and smashes to the floor. The ground around us shakes with the force and the mage smiles at me as he charges up another blast of energy in his hands, veins protruding from his neck. It is me he is coming for.

As I scramble to my feet, I realise I am out of cover and weaponless. The mage draws his arm back and growls at me, his eyes bulging as though they threaten to drop from their sockets.

"Codrin will reward me handsomely for your heads!" he screams as he fires a blast straight at me. I brace myself for the impact but it does not arrive. I hear it make contact with something in front of me, as though an invisible wall protects me.

"Jordell," I growl, "you can't keep using your magic!"

Another blast of energy hits the barrier Jordell has cast. His arms are outstretched in front of him and his sleeve lowers, revealing his wounded arm. I am shocked to see the veins tracking further up his arm at an accelerated pace as he casts his spell.

"Jordell, you need to stop, you can't sustain this!"

"I will do what I must to protect you!"

Another blast of energy hits against the barrier and the black veins crawl further up Jordell's arm and out of sight. He grimaces with pain as he deflects the magic.

Ahead of us, Yaelor grabs a dagger from one guard's corpse and rushes forward, throwing it wildly at the mage. His focus switches from me to her and he steps to the side, dodging the blade with inhuman speed.

He grimaces in pain and anger as he draws on more magic, then unfurls a blast at Yaelor. I am already moving towards her as fast as I can. I dive towards her, knocking her sideways. The blast of magic crashes into my shoulder and a searing pain engulfs my side. I slam onto the ground and writhe about in excruciating pain. The blast of magic has burnt through my clothes and seared my skin.

"Argh!" I cry out in pain as Jordell rushes toward me.

The mage grins maniacally but Yaelor is quickly upon him. She slams a rock against the side of his head and he drops to the floor. My vision begins to blur from the pain of the blast, but I can see Yaelor raising the rock above her head and bringing it down onto him, over and over again.

"You will be okay, Laith, you are going to be okay," Jordell tells me, but the pain sears deeply into my bones.

"It – it burns!"

"Yaelor, we must move quickly." Jordell rests his hand on my head. "His body is going into shock." Jordell's hand starts to glow as he prepares his magic.

"No!" I will not have his affliction worsen because of me.

The world around me darkens as I feel myself slip into an unconsciousness that seeks to relieve me from my agony.

12

JORDELL

We reach late afternoon as I desperately seek our arrival to the Forest of Opiya. Laith remains unconscious, sprawled out across the back of Yaelor's horse. I fear for him, I fear for the damage that the mage has done to him. The fact that the powerful blast did not tear a hole through his chest only speaks to the inexperience of the mage that attacked us.

The guard used some form of elixir to unlock magic and start throwing spells at us. Just how in the world is this possible? How has Morgana managed to harness such raw power that enables non-magic casters to wield power? For I feel certain that Morgana is behind this. I have no doubt her experiments have continued in the years since we left the Forest of Opiya.

As we ride, I look down into my satchel at the two vials I found when we searched the dead. Each of the guards was carrying a vial, but only two of the bottles survived the fight. The dark liquid has the consistency of blood, but its colouring is almost black. One thing is for certain: when we reach our destination, I need to examine the contents of these vials carefully. The gods only know what is inside or how the concoctions have come to be.

The rest of the afternoon's ride delivers us from the woodlands into wild plains, leaving us easy to spot. That said, we can't allow our horses to sprint the entire way. To push them too hard would lead them to an unnecessary death. The grass beneath us is long and lush, and wildflowers prosper within the green, peppering the ground with reds, oranges, purples, and yellows.

The way power surged through that guard was like nothing I have ever seen. Time is of the essence: Laith's skin is burnt and bloodied, dark traces of magic fraying the edges of the blast as if it has tattooed his skin. His body is folded limply over the back of the horse, and I do not know how long we have before the wound claims him.

I roll my sleeve up and look at the corrupted veins that crawls up my arm, worried about the similarity to Laith's wound.

Yaelor rides beside me at a trot as we allow our horses a small break from the intermittent galloping across the plains. We have been sure to stop to allow them to eat and drink but they have barely rested since our encounter in the woodlands. The sun has borne down on us most of the day, especially harsh given the time of year. Now, evening approaches, offering us a reprieve.

"Your thoughts torture you," Yaelor states, riding alongside me.

"It will not be long until we reach the forest. When we arrive, we will finally be able to find the rest that we so desperately seek."

"You care for him, don't you?" Yaelor has ridden delicately the last two days, ensuring that Laith remains as comfortable as one can be when sprawled out over the back of a horse.

A lump forms in my throat. "I have grown fond of him, yes," I answer. "We have been through a lot together, he and I. I have come to love him in a way that a father loves a son." I only speak these words as he remains unconscious. These are not words or thoughts that I have ever shared with him in open conversation.

"If anything were to happen to him, I do not know how I would manage. He has a kind heart, one that is rare to find in this world. He holds honour like no other person I have ever met." I stare up at rising full moon above, purple light surrounding it as it sinks low onto the horizon. Faint stars are peppered around it, beginning to emerge, the sky itself clear of any darkened clouds. It is a stark contrast to my mood, which is black as tar.

I feel angry that Laith is injured, frustrated that the guard was willing to sacrifice his body to wield magic and kill us.

"How did you two meet?" Yaelor asks me.

"We met in Askela," I tell her. "Jareb had sent his men in pursuit of me after I discovered the atrocities they were committing in the deepest depths of the dungeon." I shudder at the memories of witnessing Morgana torture two prisoners as she transferred a wound from one to another. I can only begin to imagine how far she has come with her magic since our paths last crossed.

"As I made my escape, the guards caught up with me. Morgana wanted me dead. My path happened to stumble across Laith's, who in turn had been sent by Vireo to find me and bring me back to the forest to heal his friend. Laith fought against the guards with me, and between the two of us we were able to escape and make our way back to Vireo's camp."

I cast my eyes over Laith and smile as I think back over that day. The skill he showed with a sword was far better than anyone his age I had ever seen, his bravery far exceeding others of his age group. "I was fond of him straight away. He has an ability to really speak some truths to people whether they want to hear it or not. You can always count on him to do the right thing."

"He seems like a good man, a good friend to have. I have never had anyone defend me in that way before, to put their life in danger to protect someone they barely know. I understand the bravery you speak of."

"It can, at times, cross the line of stupidity. It is the valour that he shows which makes him so endearing, which makes me feel a sense of pride I thought I would never have for another. Levanthria has grown to be a cruel place and Laith just wants to make it better for others. He wants the suffering to end."

"Why did you leave the safety of the forest? Why would you travel so far away from it?" Yaelor asks, her focus solely on the words that I speak. It is nice to share a conversation with her.

"I shared a vision with the sorceress, Morgana. She wishes to cheat her death, to alter the future, and I have seen the aftermath. Laith and I seek an artefact embedded in stone that can end a war before it starts."

Yaelor looks puzzled but allows me to continue.

"That boy has grown into a man whilst we have travelled together, and even he does not know how important his role is in what's to come."

"That sounds like a heavy burden to bear." Yaelor is distant as she speaks, as if she is struggling to find words, her eyes vacant as she rides. "Morgana killed my father, but I am not a true Barbaraq. I was taken as a child. True-blood Barbaraq women cannot bear children, so they take women and children as their own and nurture them before they mate and produce their bloodlines."

I am shocked to discover that she is not a true Barbaraq.

"Children are taken, and as they grow older, they are gifted to warriors so that they can mate. Once they are grown and have borne children, the wife of the warrior kills them in ritual that long outdates many others."

I have so many questions that I wish to ask, but I do not know where to start. It sounds as though her people as she calls them are even more savage than I realised. "What about those children?"

"Barbaraq girls undergo a ritual in adolescence that stops them from bearing children. My people only mate with women who are taken from the villages they storm. It is how Akssuh wills it." She looks at the sinking sun as she mentions her god's name.

In truth I cannot get my head around the logic of how the Barbaraqs act.

"Are you married?" I ask, curious to find out.

"No. My father was hard to please. He saw that no warrior was fit to be my mate. I will avenge his death at the hands of –" she pauses for a moment and as sadness creeps into her eyes, I can't help but feel that I am not getting the full story – "I will see that Morgana meets her end at the tip of my blade."

I smile. "That is something that we can both agree on." I see no exit from the war other that Morgana's death. Her thoughts are warped and cruel, and I fear that she is too far gone to seek any form of redemption.

Yaelor laughs as we continue our ride. "Who would have thought that I would end up here on this day, riding towards an enchanted forest with a young warrior unconscious on the back of my horse."

"I had a similar conversation with Laith before our paths

crossed. I will say the same as I did to him: it is not the final destination we should focus on but the path that we walk to get there."

"Tell me, how is it that you came to be so wise?"

A gentle breeze pushes against us as the weather changes to a colder climate brought on by the arriving night sky.

I laugh. "I read a lot of books."

Ahead of us, I spot the high canopy of pine trees, the sun sitting high above them as if the Goddess Opiya herself watches over them, giving the needles of the trees an almost magical bluish-green glow. A glow I recognise as our destination.

"Over there." I point out to the horizon ahead of us. "It's the Forest of Opiya. We are here."

13

JORDELL

" *I believe not all cursed creatures of this world have a truly dark heart, many are forged by the tragic events of their life. If my research is correct then I think that if certain conditions are met that these curses can be reversed. Take the beast of Bragoa for example, no one knows what deal the monster made with the gods to garner their power. All that is known that if you would be either a brave man or a stupid one to frequent the lake whilst wearing the colours of Askela.*"

ASHOLA JURIN, *Monsters of the world Volume IV, 179 KR*

AS WE APPROACH the outer edge of the forest, I am overcome with varying emotions. Relief is the main one that I hang onto. I find it ironic that I have come back to this place seeking safety despite knowing the dangers that may await inside. How the gods wield our fates in mysterious ways.

"Who goes there!" a short, hostile voice greets us from within the trees.

It causes me surprise and I pull on the mane of my horse to bring it to a stop. I am unable to see into the shroud of darkness in the outer edge of the trees. The final remnants of daylight only grant us enough clemency to see the open lands around us.

Yaelor reaches for her sword but I place my hand out to allay her fears.

"We come in search of Vireo."

Two men come out from the darkness, their bows drawn and aimed at us. It takes me a second to recognise one of them but when I do, I become encased in happiness from seeing a familiar face.

"Killian? Killian, old boy! Is that you?"

The older of the two men lowers his bow. "Jordell? What the blazes are you doing coming here at this time of night? You're lucky not to have a body filled with arrows!"

I drop down from my horse, my joints cracking as I land on the ground. I offer my hand to Killian who gladly shakes it in return. In my haste, I offer my afflicted arm, and Killian's tight grip sends a shock of pain through it all the way to my shoulder. I reel in pain and pull back gingerly.

"What is it, Jordell, what has happened to you?" Killian looks concerned, his face barely visible under the thick grey beard he now possesses. His hair is equally thick and grey, dropping down to his shoulders.

"I am fine, but Laith needs a healer urgently," I tell him. There is no time to waste with pleasantries.

"Come, let's get you back to camp."

As we move through the forest, I am not greeted with the autumnal colours of the woodlands. Instead, all the trees and their leaves remain vibrant. Different shades of green provide a canopy above, the gaps in the trees granting a near perfect level of light for the time of day. The oaky smell mixed with fresh grass and floral undertones is refreshing, and I swear for a moment I can smell fresh honey. The fragrance sets my stomach off with a deep growl, which brings about a laugh from Killian as he leads the way. It is good to see an old friend and a friendly face.

"Who's the other person with you?" Killian asks.

"This is Yaelor. She has proven to be a skilled warrior. If not for her, the mage we crossed paths with may have ended us." I look over my shoulder at Yaelor, whose face tells me she is in awe of what she sees around us.

"She carries strange markings, is she not from these lands?"

"I don't forsee that being an issue, Killian, do you?" Although she has been raised by the Barbaraqs, I feel there is every chance that she was taken from these lands. Given the age that she was taken, she may not be able to remember where she came from.

"Here we are," Killian announces.

I am taken aback at what I see before me. Three children run past, giggling whilst chasing one another. One of them taps their hand on the shoulder of another, then turns to run away in glee. Their green and brown clothing appears to have been fashioned from the trees themselves, the cotton they used likely farmed from these lands. If they were to stand in the trees for long enough, I am sure they would blend in with the trees.

"Very clever," I smile to myself as I realise that this is the very intent of the clothing they wear, to camouflage in their surroundings. Next my eyes are drawn to the vast crops which appear to have been set up on the outer edges of the camp. Men, women, and children tend to neat in rows that go back further into the gaps between the trees. Large green carrot tops protrude from the soil, and I wonder just how big the carrots are underneath.

Aubergines, larger than I have ever seen, are being collected and carried away, likely the meal for the day. What I thought was a thin cluster of trees turns out to be corn, reaching far higher than the other crops and threatening to breach the canopy above us.

"These crops, they have come such a long way from when I was last here." The memory of planting the first batch of seeds that Vireo and Gillam recovered from the Great Temple floats to the forefront of my mind.

"True, the crops grow like no other place in Levanthria, and far quicker. But you already know that. We have just shown people how to tend to the crops, we think it's the nutrients in the soil. We take it as a sign from the forest that they approve of us being here. After all, Vireo is incredibly strict about the rule that we only take out of the forest what we ourselves put in."

Killian's words draw a smile from me as he repeats the very advice I once imparted on Vireo. I take comfort in knowing that the once selfish man has taken to my guidance and imparted it onto others.

"You have a resourceful community," Yaelor says. "My people would be envious."

If the crops are something to behold, then I am in awe when we reach the main part of the camp. Wooden huts, tepees, and tents line the gaps between the trees, all made from produce from the forest. Some sit on the ground while others are built into the trees above. It is truly a magnificent splendour to behold. I cannot count the number of huts, tents, and hammocks that I see, all of varying sizes and designs.

People stand and talk, sharing stories with one another in conversation. Laughter rings out between people while others go about their day. Men and women carry harvested crops. One small family carries a pile of clothes into a gap in the trees. I have no idea where this leads, but can only assume it is a place to wash their clothes.

Then the senses in my nose explode. I take in a large sniff, my gargling belly threatening to eat itself from hunger.

"Is that bread?" I exclaim. A joy I have not experienced for so longs sends a warm feeling down my spine and my cheeks sting, my smile is that wide. Killian casts me a proud grin, one that matches my own. Vireo has somehow managed to create an entire community within the forest, its numbers far exceeding those from when I was here last.

"We have a visitor!" Killian announces as we approach the centre of the encampment. A base fire sits in the centre, and I recognise the stones circle that we made years ago.

It is truly amazing to see how things have evolved in our absence. I recognise a couple of faces but no one I would know the name of. Then Vireo turns to face us. He looks confused by our sudden appearance, but his frown is quickly replaced by a wild grin.

He still wears that green cloak, but it is not as tattered and torn as before; it looks like Vireo has carried out some repair work on it. Underneath his cloak he wears hide pants and a shirt decorated to help him blend in with the trees. His hair is much longer now, slicked back and tied neatly behind his head. Despite living in the wild, his dark beard is groomed well, and he is still tending to his appearance as he used to.

"Jordell, old friend!" Vireo steps forward and pats my horse on the neck. "Welcome back to Verusha," he says.

I cast him a smile and dismount, this time offering my good arm for a handshake. Vireo smiles as he shakes it firmly. "You finally came up with a name for this place. It has been a long ride," I tell him, "and I have much I need to discuss with you."

"Jordell, is that you?" I recognise her soft voice in an instant, and I beam as Gillam joins us in the centre of camp. Her hair is tied back tightly, and she wears dark leathers complete with a crimson cloak. I can't help but notice that she walks with a heavy limp as she approaches. Her hazel eyes beam as she embraces me, and I am surprised by this display of affection; I remember Gillam to be as cold as ice. I accept her hug and pat her gently on her back.

"It is so good to see you on your feet, my dear. I feared that you may not walk again after your fall."

"I'm sure your magic had something to do with it." She smiles. "That, and the remedies you left for me. I think this is the best that it will heal, though."

Gillam's joyous mood is short-lived and her face transforms into a picture of worry when she sees Laith unconscious on the back of the horse. "What's happened? Is he okay?" she says in a panicked state. I did not realise that she cared for him. Gillam rushes to Laith and brushes his long blond hair back to reveal his stubbled face.

"He has been caught with a blast of magic fighting a mage. We need to tend to his wounds, and he needs to rest."

Gillam looks over him with concern and rightfully so. "Killian, help me get him to the healer's tent."

"I'll stay with him," Yaelor announces as she dismounts her horse. She helps Killian and Gillam carry Laith down. Two other villagers bring a makeshift stretcher over and they lift Laith onto it. He groans in pain as they move him.

"Follow me." Gillam leads the way as Yaelor and Killian follow behind her, carrying Laith.

"Is there nothing you can do with your magic?" Vireo asks.

"I wanted to use my power to help Laith but in true fashion, he forbade it. I am afraid my body grows weary." Then I place my hands on both his shoulders and look into his eyes with pride. "Vireo, what you have achieved here is truly outstanding." He has come such a long way from his days of acting as a debt collector for the Crown, since our paths first crossed in Askela.

"It has been a hard few years since you left us, I am not going to lie. But these people have been committed to the cause that we now have. To our new sustained life in the forest. Our numbers have swelled as word has reached farther than Askela. Those that want to join us are welcome. Free of the burden that King Athos places on his people, we do not acknowledge his rule here, nor would we accept it. It is thanks to the people of this commune that we prosper, with each person contributing in some way, however best they can. This is all I ask of them. That, and to only take –"

"- from the forest what we put in," I finish his words, laughing. "It is pleasing to know that my words have remained with you."

"Well, it has worked."

There is a rustle in the nearby trees, followed by a growl. My heart sinks as panic sets in, and I draw my hand to my blade instinctively. Strangely, no one else does the same. Instead, Vireo laughs and turns to face the bear-sized wolfaire that is bounding towards him. It snarls, its crown pointing down to reveal its large, curling horns on either side of its head. When it reaches us, Vireo dives forward and wraps his arm around the beast's thick neck. To my surprise, it drops to the ground on its side and Vireo begins to ruffle its fur.

"Recognise him?" Vireo laughs as he drags his fingers across the creature's side, giving it a playful scratch. It growls in appreciation, then lies across the ground and lets out a large yawn, revealing its teeth. It is the wolfaire that helped Vireo when he first arrived here, the wolfaire that Vireo had once rescued.

I smile. "He is even bigger than I remember."

"Shadow likes to sneak up on me, it's become a game of ours." Vireo pats him on the head one more time. Recognizing a dismissal, Shadow climbs up to his feet and wanders off into the trees. "Do you care to walk with me, Jordell?"

Pain lingers in my arm, the tips of my fingers feeling as though they are burning. As much as I have looked forward to a catch-up with Vireo, I'd be lying if I said I wasn't distracted by the constant pain in my arm, and the extent of Laith's injury.

Vireo leads the way. As I walk beside him, I can't help but notice that his body language has changed since I first arrived. The arrogant swagger he used to possess seems to have faded, replaced by a calmness as he places his hand behind his back while he walks.

"It seems to have proven most useful having the wolfaires around to help keep other creatures away from the camp."

"So it would seem." Vireo's mood darkens as we speak. "But it is not all good news in regard to our camp."

"What is it, Vireo?"

"The forest has accepted us, but we are not alone here. Dangers lurk in parts of the forest that remain unexplored."

"I remember all too well the ogre that attacked us in the depths of these woods." We barely survived, and if not for the wolfaires defending us, we may not have.

Vireo stops by a row of painted sticks protruding from the ground that seem to be marking the boundary of the camp.

"We are in conflict with another race, one which has lived far deeper in the forest for far longer than us." He turns to me, his face carrying a burden I did not expect.

"They are called the fae and as far as I can tell, they are less than pleased with us making camp in this forest."

14

LAITH

As my eyes drowsily open, the light entering the room causes them to sting as though they have been filled with vinegar. Raising my hand, I block as much of the light as I can as I take in my surroundings. My head aches tremendously but it pales in comparison to what I feel in my shoulder.

I remember the fight in the woodlands, the guard who could wield magic after drinking an elixir, but I do not recall what happened after.

I groan loudly in pain and shuffle myself to a seated position, surprised to find myself in a bed. I grit through the dull pain, but I suddenly find myself increasingly dizzy and the room shakes around me.

Then I take in the small room. The ramshackle walls appear to be fashioned from branches and sticks, light forcing its way in through the gaps.

Where am I?

There is a musty smell in the air that is earthy, a potent mixture of other ingredient, too. I glance down at my shoulder.

The fragrance of the remedy used to treat my shoulder greets me, no doubt something that Jordell has concocted. My shoulder is bandaged, however, which I find strange; I do not recall Jordell having bandages in his supplies. My chest and shoulder are bound tightly, and I grumble to myself in pain as I rotate my shoulder to get an understanding of my injury. There doesn't seem to be any lasting damage, for which I am grateful.

A light cough startles me and my heart skips a beat. I turn my head quickly to see Yaelor sitting on a chair in the corner of the room.

"Where are we?" I ask, clearing my throat. My voice is hoarse, and my mouth feels as dry as a desert.

"Jordell managed to get us to the forest that we spoke of, we are in the camp," Yaelor says, her face stony. "How do you feel?"

"Like I have fallen off a cliff." I search around the room, still confused by the hut that I find myself in. The last time I was here, no such things were in camp, only a makeshift shelter fashioned out of the back of a horse's cart. "How long have I been unconscious?"

Yaelor stands and stretches out her arms and back, audible cracks erupting from her joints. "The sun has set four times since we arrived here."

"You've been here the whole time?" I ask.

Yaelor frowns at my question. "You saved my life, Laith. The least I can do is watch over you whilst you make your recovery."

It surprises me that she has done this, but I am grateful for the kindness. "Thanks," I say awkwardly.

"Do you feel able to get up? They have left some clean clothes for you." Yaelor picks up a pile of clothes and my boots and places them at the bottom of my bed.

"I guess I need to try at some point." As I raise my cover to swing my legs out of bed, I realise that I am naked, and I quickly pull my quilt back on.

"What is it?" Yaelor asks tilting her head to the side.

I find myself stumbling for words, a flash of heat burning my cheeks. "It appears that I am naked."

"Why are you so nervous about being naked? Your body is the only gift truly given by the gods," she says assertively.

Given the rather immodest attire that Yaelor wears, her attitude towards being without clothes does not surprise me. What she walks around in would barely pass as undergarments in Askela.

Yaelor raises an eyebrow. "Is there an issue that causes you not to have confidence?"

I look down towards my groin before clicking what she is insinuating. "No!" I answer far too quickly. "It's just, I have never been in this position before. You know, not having any clothes on whilst in the company of a woman."

Yaelor does not seem to fully understand what I am trying to explain. She folds her arms tightly in front of her. "Well, are you going to get dressed?"

I glance from Yaelor to the opening of the hut, but she looks back at me blankly, not understanding my hint.

"Can I have a minute, you know, to get dressed?" I ask. Subtlety well and truly has left our conversation.

Yaelor scowls. "I do not understand why you feel so awkward about your skin. I will wait outside if that helps."

"If you could." I nod, the burning in my cheeks flashing even hotter than before.

Yaelor exits the hut and I drag myself up to my feet, a little unsteady at first but that is to be expected if I have been unconscious for so long. I gingerly get myself dressed, struggling with my pants and boots without the full use of my left arm. As I place the cotton shirt over my head, I savour the feeling against my skin. The clothes smell clean, and they are not torn and frayed like those I would have arrived in. The fabric feels like a luxury I have long forgotten, but one I welcome the return of.

Taking in a deep breath, I head to the doorway of the hut to find Yaelor standing on a wooden walkway. To my surprise, we are suspended high up in the trees. People bustle around underneath us, going about their daily tasks. I am taken aback at how this camp, once inhabited by five of us, has transformed into a vibrant community.

"Laith, you are awake!"

I turn to see Gillam moving swiftly for me, though she is limping slightly. She doesn't offer me an opportunity to return greetings before she wraps her arms around me. Her squeeze aggravates my shoulder, but I dare not say anything. I am surprised by the show of affection from her usually stony person. She is a skilled, ruthless assassin trained for the shadows. Perhaps being in the forest for so long has softened her rock-hard exterior.

"Hi, Gillam."

She pins my arms to a point where I cannot return the hug or even pat her on the back. "Gillam, my shoulder," I say when I can't tolerate the pain any further.

"Sorry." She smiles and looks at me with her deep hazel eyes, her pale skin catching in the beams of light the force their way through the canopy above us. She steps back from me, and I breathe a sigh of relief as the pain reduces in my shoulder, although it still throbs wildly. Gillam places her hands gently on each of my arms. "You have grown so much! You are not so much the scrawny boy you were when you left with Jordell."

A familiar flame fills my cheeks as I feel them redden, something that is happening far too much today for my liking. "I, erm, thanks." It's all I can muster, and I kick myself for not knowing how to react. "Is that Killian?" I opt for a diversionary tactic, recognising his ruffled hair and beard down below. "And is that –"

"His daughter? Yes," Gillam answers my question before I even finish asking it, her gaze lingering momentarily on Yaelor who stands quietly by my side.

Killian tends to some soil, digging holes which his daughter who then puts the seeds in. She is still a child but considerably bigger since the last time I saw her. Once she puts the seeds in, Killian seals them with dirt. When he looks up and sees me watching them, he raises a hand and casts me a joyous wave. It is so warming to see so many familiar faces, a comfort that I have missed. It feels like home.

I spend a moment savouring the view, embracing the happiness that fills my body like the unwrapping of a gift. This community is something special. Something that could lead as an example for how Levanthria should be governed. People working for one another, supporting one another, truly equal.

I close my eyes and listen to the birds in song, acknowledging each varying tone. I listen to the hustle and bustle of the people below, the children playing, people laughing.

A shrill scream pierces my ears like an arrow, causing the hair on my arms to stand on end. The tranquillity is suddenly replaced by chaos. Children are quickly ushered inside, trapdoors in the ground raised as people disappear inside them like a well-rehearsed play.

"Come with me." Gillam sets of down the walkway and I quickly follow with Yaelor trailing behind me. My heart beats like a drum as we navigate the walkway to the lower level until we reach the ground. Gillam sets off at speed, a dagger clutched in each hand. She moves swiftly enough that I didn't even notice her remove them. The area is clear within moments, with only those that can bear arms remaining. They take up defensive positions around the camp, armed with swords, makeshift shields, and spears.

Gillam continues to skip over the terrain, and as we approach the outer edges of the camp, I see a small group consisting of Killian, Jordell, and Vireo standing over a body. The man is sprawled out across the ground, three arrows protruding from his chest.

A murderer within the camp?

"Fucking fae!" Gillam curses, and I am confused by her statement.

"What are the fae?" I ask as I pull up next to her.

"The main cause of our problems right now."

15

JORDELL

"He must have overstepped the boundaries. For them to bring him back and leave him here tells me that they are sending us a message." Vireo crouches by the side of the body and inspects the dead man. He grips one of the arrows and pulls it from the torso to inspect it further. "The way these arrowheads are shaped, they are definitely crafted by fae. Three arrows tells me they are becoming more and more frustrated with our presence and passing into their land."

As I examine the arrow myself, my eyes are drawn to the wound left behind. The blackened skin on the outer edge of the punctures looks familiar.

"Magic," I whisper under my breath. Then I turn to Laith. It is good to see him back on his feet. "Show me your shoulder," I tell him.

Laith rotates his shoulder and winces, the colour draining from his face. He sees it, too.

As he lowers his tunic, I grab hold of the coarse fabric and pull it downwards. The burn itself has healed, but the blackened edge is as dark as ever. It is as I thought. It matches the burn on this dead villager's chest.

"How can this be?" I mutter my thoughts aloud again. "The two injuries match." I point towards Laith whose muscled shoulder is on display. "I believe that the magic used against us by those guards was fae magic."

"Are you sure?" Vireo asks. He kneels next to the dead man and traces his fingers over the blackened wounds that killed him.

"I am as sure as night and day. Have you attempted to discuss terms with them, Vireo?" I ask. "Maybe diplomacy will aid in this situation. Especially if we have a common enemy."

Vireo snaps the arrow in his hand and throws it into the dirt in frustration. "It is futile, discussing anything with them. Those magical creatures will not let us anywhere near them. We have too many dead bodies to testify to that. I have told them, I have warned our people not to cross the boundaries, yet some of them insist. Is it any wonder they end up losing their lives? It is not something I can take responsibility for if people choose to be ignorant of my warnings."

"What if they attack in retaliation for overstepping the boundaries?" Laith asks, pulling his tunic back up.

"I do not think they seek to attack the camp, otherwise they would have done so already," Vireo answers, staring into the shadows beyond the trees. "Verusha is well-defended. They have never crossed into our side. Gillam, Killian, can you see to it that Cruwis is granted a proper burial?"

"Of course." Along with some other people, they help lift the dead body and carry him away back to the main camp. Vireo walks towards Laith and offers him his hand. "It is good to see you up and about, we have been worried about you."

Laith smiles as he shakes his hand and places his free hand

on top. "It is good to see you too, Vireo. Thank you for helping me recover from my injuries."

Vireo looks down at the firm handshake Laith gives him. "This is your home boy, although looking at you now, it does not feel right to call you this. You have grown into those ears of yours." He grins.

It is nice to see the two together and not fighting, as used to be the case.

"What now? Do we need to send out a hunting party?" Laith asks.

"No, that would be foolish. If we send out a group, they would likely not return. We need to learn from this and move on. Our people need to understand not to cross these boundaries." Vireo kicks some dried earth over the pool of blood that lies on the ground between us.

"I do believe that Laith has a point," I intervene. "But to go into those trees in a confrontational manner would lead to certain death and a further breakdown in relations." I think I understand what we must do, what I must do. I have never met fae before, but I have read plenty about them. They fae are referenced throughout the spellbook I have in my possession." I reach into my satchel and remove the tome. I swear I could recite the pages from front to back, I have read it that many times.

I have been searching through the pages every night, but the information about the fae has not meant much to me up until now. When Vireo told me of them being present, I took it as a sign from the gods. To learn that they still exist means that they may have some much-needed information that could aid us on our quest.

"Fae folk have a very particular set of magic that they wield, linked to the elements of the earth. The magic used against us was as though lightning had been pulled from the sky. This book references fae tied to the wind walkers."

"What are you saying?" Vireo asks impatiently.

"Wind walkers wield that magic." I reach back into my satchel and remove one of the elixirs that I took from the guards we defeated in the nearby woodlands. "I have listened to your talk of the fae, and I believe that somehow these elixirs are linked to them. The fae are magical beings. I am a spell-caster. Maybe that will grant me some clemency. If I can get close enough, I can ask to speak to their leader."

"Go in alone?" Laith scowls. "That would be madness, you can't go in there without support, without me."

"It must be me. According to this book, the fae believe magic to be a gift from the gods. They will soon see that I will not bring about any harm to their kind."

I understand Laith's concern, but I believe I am the only spellcaster here. I can only hope that through being able to wield magic, they will at least listen to me. "I will do what I must. I have questions about these elixirs that I feel they may be able to answer. Maybe I will be able to bring about some form of understanding between your camp and theirs. And hopefully they will be able to give me something to fully heal that wound of yours, Laith."

"No, you can't go in there alone, Jordell. I won't allow it. My wound is fine. It's healing!"

I am as uncomfortable with the situation as he is, but I see no other way. "I am not asking for permission from either of you." My eyes dart from Vireo to Laith and back again. "I am of my own mind, and I feel this is the soundest plan we have right now."

"Or we could simply remind people not to cross the bound-aries," Vireo points out, annoyed.

I shake my head. "If the blade we seek exists, it will be

embedded in stone within the deepest parts of this forest. I must go either way."

Laith's face reddens with anger, but I know when he calms, he will understand and respect my choices. "So that's it then? You're going without any consideration for what we think? I can't even go with you?" He crosses his arms, and for a moment I think he might actually stomp his feet.

"I need you to respect the decision I have made."

"You do what you want then. I guess I will just sit around here with the others!" Laith raises his voice before turning and storming off back towards the camp. Yaelor stands caught in the middle of the argument, then follows Laith. I do not like being in conflict with him, but I would rather this than lead him to his death.

"I will keep an eye on him," Vireo reassures me. "Now, old friend, are you sure you want to do this?"

"It is more a case of need than want," I correct. "I hope to see you soon, Vireo."

"You mad bastard." With this, Vireo smiles and heads off back to camp, leaving me on my own.

Laith had every reason to call it madness, but this Great War is far closer than we care to wish.

I turn towards the thick trees ahead of me. Silence greets me as if the forest has stripped all sound to allow me to gather my thoughts. I take a deep breath. "You old fool," I mutter to myself.

Then I take my firsts steps into the forest, beyond the boundaries.

16

LAITH

"*I find it laughable that the Great Temple seek to put one of their own on the throne. They are not happy with the power they lost under King Athos Almerion's reign. We need to act with due-diligence if we are to ensure that one of of our own are not pushed aside by Lord Myrion Sand.*"

LETTER to the court of Byron, Coratios Vex, 255 KR

MY TOE THROBS as I kick a rock in anger, which skips across the dirt before bouncing off the side of a nearby tree. The sharp sting distracts me only for a second before I let out a growl of frustration. Why has he gone off alone? How can he be so stupid? It is one thing to put himself in harm's way, but to do so without consideration for my thoughts or feelings on the matter irks me even further. My hands tremble as I march back towards camp, my anger rising to a point I have not experienced since last being here. Yaelor tails behind me in silence.

"To blazes with this damned forest, with this blasted quest." I curse the air, my jaw tense as I struggle with Jordell's decision. As we enter camp, people look sheepish, having heard me call out in frustration. I pass Gillam who is relaying the message that it is safe for the members of the camp to come out. Those that hid in the trees and underground are returning to the surface, calm and collected. They have definitely gone through this before, then. Those who stood guard are helping one another stack their weapons back on the weapon racks scattered across camp.

Exhaling deeply, I try and settle myself, but in truth I have never felt this level of anger towards Jordell.

"You need to calm down, Laith," Gillam grabs me by my good arm and pulls me back towards her. "Are you listening to me?"

I try and pull my arm free, but her grip tightens and pulls me back even harder this time.

Reluctantly, I turn to face her. "He made his decision. He made it without a care for what the rest of us thought. I would have gladly gone with him, he needs protection. He should not be out there alone." My voice is hoarse and my throat burns with my words. "He made his decision too quickly and in haste, something he has always warned me against. I have been by his side every day for over three years. For him to leave like that tells me that he has little regard for me."

"Come now." Gillam scowls, looking less than impressed with my attitude. "Do you not think you are being a little over-dramatic?"

"I agree with Gillam, Jordell is wise enough to make his own decisions," Yaelor puts her coin in.

"What would you know? You've only been with us for a short time." As soon as the words leave my mouth, I instantly regret them. Yaelor has been nothing but a help since she joined our party, and she does not deserve to meet the brunt of my frustration. "I'm sorry, I –"

Yaelor's fist greets my cheek. My neck snaps to the side, and my cheek starts to pulsate with a dull, throbbing pain.

"*Vura!*" she curses me in her tongue and spits on the ground. As she barges past me, her shoulder connects with my injured one, causing me to wince. What a fool I have acted.

Gillam puts her hands on her hips. "Well, that was fucking stupid." Those around us seem to be trying in vain to appear busy, and not at all invested in the spectacle that has just unfolded.

"I am in no mood for a lecture, Gillam." Blood collects in my mouth and I spit it on the floor. I just wish to be left alone, to collect my thoughts and come up with a plan.

"Tough shit," she fires back, "because you are going to get one, cause and effect. You act like a prick, and you will be treated like one." She walks past me, barging into my other shoulder.

"Walk with me." She places her hands behind her back and walks slowly and calmly through the centre of camp. She stops for a second before looking over her shoulder towards me. When her eyes meet mine, a sense of shame comes over me and I can't help but drop my gaze to the ground. "I will not ask again."

I am not keen on the threatening undertone to her voice, and I am all too familiar with how good she is with a blade, not to mention the things she has done to Vireo and Lek as punishment for getting on the wrong side of her over the years.

Like a scolded pup with its tail between its legs, I follow her.

"Do you know that while you were unconscious, Yaelor did not leave your side? She remained with you from the moment you arrived, to the moment that you woke up. Do you know how hard it is to find commitment like that? Yet you spit in her face like a petulant child."

We walk out of the other side of camp to a more secluded area of the forest, and I can only imagine she has brought me here so no one else will hear the bollocking I am to receive. "There was me thinking you left a boy and returned a man. I am disappointed in you."

"I am sorry, I didn't mean –"

Gillam raps me across the other cheek.

"I did not bring you here to draw an apology from you. I brought you here to calm you down and try and make you see sense. It is up to you how you react."

The irony that she wants me to remain calm whilst simultaneously striking me is enough.

"I do not want to hear words from you. In this moment, I only ask you to listen to the advice and guidance I am about to impart." She takes a step away from me and raises both her hands. "Do this and I promise not to strike you again."

I feel like a child being schooled but it is no less than I deserve for the way I have behaved.

"I am listening." The words fall out of my mouth like I'm a petulant babe.

"The sooner you realise that sometimes people will make choices that you do not agree with, the better. Otherwise, you will push everyone away from you." She rests her hands on the hilts of her daggers, and for a moment I wonder if she would draw them on me, her face still reddened with anger of her own.

"When we first ended up in this forest, I wanted to kill Vireo. I was tempted on more than one occasion to act on my darkened thoughts. After all, his selfishness had cost us our home, our land, and any honour we held within the higher rankings amongst Askela. I lost everything because that oaf could not keep his dick in his pants."

I listen to her words as intently as I can, both my cheeks, shoulder, and toe throbbing as wild as the leaves that blow in the breeze. I avoid her eyes, the sense of shame still hanging over me like an unwanted shadow.

"It was his selfish thoughts and actions that led us here. But through those decisions, through his actions, he has more than redeemed himself. And for it, he is a far better man than he once was. Although incensed at what I lost, I have come to respect the choices Vireo made. If we were allowed back in time, I would still walk the same path we have trodden."

Gillam's stern eyes turn into a smile, and she points to the camp. "Look at the good he has done, look at what he has built. I have followed Vireo into battle. He is my brother-in-arms and I would die for him. These people have chosen to follow him. These people have chosen him as their leader. Every day, he has to make decisions, every one of them running the risk of coming into quarrel with someone who does not agree. But they accept the decisions that he makes, because they trust that his intentions are for the best of everyone. Somehow that selfish man has learned to become selfless. He does it all, no matter what the burden is to him, he does it for these people."

"I understand." I have acted like an insolent child. More focused on how I felt rather than the reason why Jordell made the decision he did.

"We cannot undo the things that we have done in our past, but we can seek to learn from them and become wiser for it."

Hearing how wise Gillam sounds right now, I ponder on just how many mistakes she has made in her past. "Thank you," I say, raising my head to meet her eyes.

She casts me a smile and I appreciate the words she has

shared with me. I look around us and back to the hut where I woke up earlier. It already feels like such a long time ago.

"I guess I should find Yaelor. I owe her an apology."

"My final advice would be to maybe allow her some time before you do so. I don't know if that handsome face of yours could take another blow."

My cheeks redden again, partly from being hit and partly from Gillam's words. They burn deep like the embers spawned from coal, and I turn to hide them, finding myself embarrassed.

"I have been such a fool," I muse. I should have respected Jordell's decision. Now he is out there alone, and my last time talking with him, I was bawling at him and storming away. I can only pray that he returns safely so I can make my peace with him.

"I have no doubt you will learn from this. Remember, it is how you respond to the choices that you make. I will leave you to your thoughts." With this, Gillam brushes past me. This time her hand brushes my arm tenderly.

I sit by a nearby tree and look out at the deep, dark forest, wondering what is going to happen to Jordell and praying to the gods to favour him.

17

JORDELL

I travel northeast of the camp, or so I think. There are no pathways to follow. Vines and leaves create small pockets of walls that make it impossible to travel through, often forcing me to backtrack and find alternate routes. My lower legs are whipped and scratched by the thorns and spikes protruding from lower branches and shrubs.

The skies begin to darken as night approaches, and that is not a good thing; I am out in the open, and this deep into the forest, I dread to think what creatures are keeping their beady eyes on me. It isn't only birds that I hear. Growls of animals or beasts rumble quietly around me, but I have no idea how close to me they are. I can only hope that I find the fae before I stumble across something more deadly.

My breathing is heavy and my chest aches, a pain in my side forming from my long days walking. As tempting as it is to stop and rest, I do not want to stop. Just in case anything is stalking me.

I push a large, leaf-filled branch out of the way before allowing it to snap back into position after I pass. A flock of birds flees at the sudden noise, which startles me into a jump. My heart suddenly speeds up and I curse loudly at them as they fly off to the higher treetops. As the dark approaches, luminous mushrooms spring into life around me, acting as natural torches as I continue my journey. A soft, blue hue radiates from them, pulsating as I walk past. I stare into one and let the light calm my mind, the temptation to cut one down all too tempting. But I need to live by the guidance that I set, and to only take from the forest what we put in. I would not want to provoke the gods this far into these unknown territories.

Vines wrap around my feet. As I stumble forward, I slam my hand against the trunk of a tree to steady myself, but it slides over a sticky substance. I lose my footing and tumble to the ground, my knees cracking as I put my arms forward. I call out in pain as I use my corrupted arm to brace myself. It feels as though fire travels through my veins, and the temptation to use my magic draws me ever closer to succumbing to its will. Sweat beads on my head as I grimace from the pain, and I plant one foot on the ground before steadying myself upright once more.

I lean against the same tree my hand slipped from and pant heavily as I regather my composure, all the while searching the area around me to make sure nothing is ready to pounce. As I do this, something dawns on me, something that sends a shiver down my spine.

There is no noise, no birds in song, no grumbles or howls from the distance. Not so much as a rustling leaf. The forest has fallen completely silent, with nothing but my heavy breathing to be heard. As I search the trees around me, I am drawn to something hidden between the thick, green leaves. A pair of bone-white eyes greet me in return.

Native cries ring out from all around me, and I place myself with my back against the tree, refusing to draw upon my sword. I have found the fae, it seems. Or rather, they have found me.

I don't have time to count how many there are as I find both my arms tightly clasped at either side of me. I am lurched forward and moved from my spot to a small clearing. Fingers wrap tightly around my wrist as the fae cheer and revel in my capture.

I raise my head to get a glimpse of one of them for the first time. It is a male, his face thinner than my own. He carries a rugged jawline clean of any stubble. His skin is pale, like it is of the same milk as the moon, and his pointed ears are lined with wooden piercings. He is bare chested, revealing a body taut with muscle, and a collar of branches and leaves hangs loosely around his neck. He carries a spear which he has pointed at my chest. He does not say a word as he approaches.

As the spear tip grows closer, I notice it seems to be made of obsidian, the shiny black stone delicately carved to form a sharpened rock. More fae gather on either side of us, their skin colours varied like I am staring at the palette of an autumn woodlands. Dark brown, light brown, even lighter still as though verging on orange. Their skin shines thanks to the mushrooms that illuminate our surroundings. Some of them carry markings on their skin not too dissimilar from Yaelor's war paint. The tribal markings are etched into them like branches and leaves across their torsos and arms. One of the fae has a tree etched up his torso with the branches stretching out across his chest and up his neck.

"Please, I mean no harm." Raising my hands to either side of me, I try to communicate for the first time.

For my efforts, I am greeted with a jab of the blunt end of the spear from the fae in front of me.

"Sporenu!" The fae spits. He is the only one wearing a crest around his neck. Could this one be the leader of this group?

"Please." I lower my hands. "I come seeking an audience with your leaders. I promise that I am a friend."

The fae leans forward and takes a sharp intake of breath through his nose. Then the fae on either side of him, one male and one female, do the same. The male takes a few samples of air near my face. An oaky smell emits from them, and I can't help but wonder if this race of creatures is born of the very trees themselves.

They recoil from me, their faces a combination of shock and confusion. They push each other whilst speaking in a tongue I cannot decipher. They keep looking at me, the leader of the group listening before shaking his head.

The female rushes at me and takes another intake of my scent before looking down at my satchel. Her skin is a pale orange, her clothing derived from fabric stitched with leaves. Her face is narrow, her eyes an emerald-green colour. Her scent is sweeter than the oaky smell of the male, with floral undertones.

She reaches down to my satchel and opens it up.

"Please be careful," I ask. Not so much because of the elixir but because of the priceless spellbook that I have in my possession.

The fae woman hisses at me and bares her teeth, her hot breath pressing against my cheek. I turn from her, my heart beating that little bit faster. I hear the clinking of the vials and as I turn back, she removes them from my possession.

"I found them," I try to explain, uncertain if they understand my words. "We were attacked by people who drank these elixirs. The magic inside them, it is not natural. The person who used it was granted powers I believe to be from the wind walkers."

The chattering and hissing stop in an instant, the leader of this group looking over me in an untrusting manner. His breathing quickens, not through overexertion but through anger. The fae woman passes him one of the vials. He brings the vial level with his eyes and rotates it, its thick blackened contents the consistency of tar. The liquid has a thick viscosity and coats the glass before slowly sliding down the sides. With a delicate hand, he removes the cork of the vial and brings it closer to his face.

"No!" I call out, worried that he means to drink the elixir. "I do not know what damage drinking that liquid will do to your body!" For my warnings, I receive a jab to the side from one of the fae. A sharp pain followed by a dull ache serves as a reminder to keep quiet.

The leader does not drink the unnatural liquid. Instead, he brings the vial below his nose and sniffs it whilst whirling the contents inside, as though some sort of connoisseur. His eyes dart from the vial and fixate onto mine. He emits a low growl, his face contorting with disgust.

"Aruya!" he cries, then passes the elixir around to the others. One by one they sniff it, each time repeating the word that the leader speaks.

"Aruya! Aruya!"

They speak in hushed tones as if gossiping amongst one another. Heads bob as if in agreement over something.

"ARUYA!" the leader roars. The rest in the group raise their heads and howl, some angry, some pained, some faces confused by the discussion they are having.

"Please, I only want to help. I think this elixir is somehow linked to your people." I reach into my satchel and pull out the spell tome. "Magic lies within me, this book has helped me." As I raise the ancient leather tome into the air, my sleeve slides down and I notice the back of my hand is almost completely black. On my arm, tracking veins grow more bulbous, darker and thicker as the corruption threatens to cover my skin in its entirety.

Gasps emit from the crowded group as one by one they raise their hands and point.

"Elderu, ELDERU!" They call in unison, their voices raised in chant. The sound thunders above the canopy of the forest like the beating of a drum.

The leader rushes into my personal space, his face drawing equal with mine. I can taste the distrust in the air, the growls under his breath every bit as intimidating as I imagine he intends them to be.

"I -"

The leader flicks up his spear so that the blunt side is pointing towards me. At least I have something to be thankful for. He cracks it against the side of my head, and stars ignite in my vision with an almighty flash. The fae start to blend in with the green leaves and bark behind them. The world spins wildly, my breathing hastening until I slip away into the dark void of unconsciousness.

18

LAITH

"The tales of Gregor Yerald stretch far beyond Levanthria, it is why it is now tradition for families to leave food out for him and his Yakula. For if you are to do this during the Winterast Festival, it is believed that Gregor will bring you favour and with that a ward which will keep away demons and spirits that would seek to cause you harm."

TALES OF LEVANTHRIA, Freya Knach, Tales of Levanthria 142 KR

THE FIRE in the centre of camp provides a comforting level of warmth, and the embers crack from the fallen branches used to keep it going. A large pan sits atop the flame, its contents almost empty, the fragrant smell of vegetable soup drifting up my nose for me to savour.

"That was delicious, Killian," I exclaim, rubbing my stomach. It has been too long since I last had a belly full of food. So much so that I almost feel guilty about it. Not only was the vegetable soup filled with the most vibrant, ripened vegetables ranging from carrots, swede, parsnips, and potatoes, but there was also a cob of bread on offer, too. The meal was truly delightful. It was nice to see the people of this commune come together to help prepare the large batch before it was shared amongst everyone. Children first, then the older folk followed by everyone else.

"The recipe was one passed onto me by my wife – gods rest her soul – her mother, and her grandmother before her. The least I can do to honour her is make sure others enjoy the recipe. It also helps being a former innkeeper." Killian smiles before inspecting the large cast-iron pan, which is large enough to be mistaken for a cauldron. But then again, it has been needed to feed more than fifty people. There are two large wooden tables where everyone sits to dine together, benches sitting on either side. With the meal finished, people tend to cleaning the table, while others prepare to take the wooden bowls away to be cleaned in the nearby river.

The glow of the fire draws my focus as I sit beside Killian and a couple of others who I am not familiar with. I stew on my full stomach, a tiredness creeping over me as the night grows darker. Lanterns are placed around the huts, tents, tepees, and trees, some on the ground, some raised up in the trees. They cast a gentle light around the camp that makes it feel as though we are in a small village. In fact, I would go so far as to say that Verusha has become a true village.

The hustle and bustle of the day has dampened down to only a few moving around camp and sitting by small fires to keep warm. Plenty have taken their leave and returned to their makeshift homes, either on their own or with their families. Killian has explained that there are around ten sentries strategically placed at various points around the camp, some on the ground, some higher up. All are armed just to be on the safe side of the creatures that could quite easily enter camp.

Killian is insistent that the wolfaires keep them at bay, and given the size of Shadow, it is clear why such majestic creatures would ward away many a monster. In return, they receive food that is left out for them, although they do not always accept the vegetables, preferring to stalk wild animals.

My shoulder throbs with a dull ache and I bring my hand to it, squeezing it gently. It soothes the pain only slightly and I rotate my shoulder, grimacing as I do so before stretching my arm out.

"You okay?" Killian asks, his dark eyes flickering from the flames of the fire.

"It's just my shoulder." The discomfort has worsened throughout the day. "Shora has given me some ointment that is made from something inside this forest. She said I was to put it on before I went to sleep, to help with the pain." The healer also warned me that the reason I was to put it on at night was because of how drowsy it would make me once my skin absorbed its properties.

"Come, I know what you need." Killian slaps his hands on his knees and stands up before waving me to walk with him. He offers his hand down to me and helps me to my feet.

"Where are we going?"

"The lagoon," he answers with a wild grin. "Has no one told you about it?"

I shake my head. Although we have been here for nearly a full week, I have only been conscious today.

"It is not far from here, and it is within our boundaries." Killian sets off so I quickly follow, intrigued by this lagoon that he speaks of.

A short walk later and I am curious just how close to the

boundary edge we are, the trees thickening to where only the light from the moon guides us now.

"Some of the healers reckon the waters contain healing properties. If your shoulder is giving you grief, maybe a swim will aid your slumber. Here it is." Killian pushes his way through a thicket of trees and pulls them to one side to allow me through.

I can't help but gasp as I take in the sight: an ice-blue lagoon sits in the middle of the forest, its waters glowing turquoise. A small waterfall sits at the back, its waters cascading down the rock face that forms around the outer edge. The reflection of the moon ripples on its surface, the stars projecting as though the water casts a perfect image of the skies above.

Then I see the stars dart around, and I quickly realise these are small fish, each glowing a vibrant colour as though enchanted themselves.

"Well, here you go. You remember the route back?" Killian asks as he pats me on the back, the force of which causes me to wince in pain. "Ah, sorry about that. As I said, hop in, enjoy the soak. If anything, a wash and a relax in here should help fix you right up."

"Is it safe?"

Killian chortles before pointing into the trees. "Well, we have been here a while and I can assure you there are no beasties in these waters. We use them all the time to bathe." He motions in the direction beyond the periphery of the lagoon. "And we have people standing watch over there. I will see you back in camp." With this, Killian disappears into the trees and suddenly I feel very alone and exposed.

I stare into the waters and walk closer to them until my own reflection stares back at me. My hair is thick and greasy, my face rough with a thick stubble. I look as though I have been dragged at the foot of a horse. My eyes are puffed and baggy, my lips cracked. I notice my shoulder stoops slightly from my injury, and my cheek still bears the mark where I was struck, first by Yaelor, then by Gillam.

I find myself lost in my thoughts. I have not seen Yaelor since I was rude to her, meaning I have been unable to right my wrong. It is something I have been meaning to do. I muse on the words that Gillam imparted on me as I stare into the darkness beyond the trees. My thoughts trace to Jordell, who I can only hope is safe in this moment and that his quest soon finds him back in the safety of our camp. I close my eyes and allow the sound of the waterfall to bring me a moment of solace. It drowns out all the noises in my mind, helps bring me a moment of peace and clarity. I take in a few slow, deep breaths before opening my eyes and pinching myself at the sight of the exotic lagoon. With this, I take heed of Killian's advice and remove my boots and my clothes, leaving them in a pile by the edge of the water.

Having bathed in cold waters far too often, I have found that jumping in helps me with dealing with the initial shock. I leap forward and crash into the lagoon, and as I find myself submerged, I am pleasantly surprised. The water is warm to my skin, and as I swim to the surface, the water feels thicker than its usual consistency, which I find soothing.

When I reach the surface, I take in some air and rub my hands through my hair. I do not recall the last time I went for a swim. Killian was right. I feel myself relaxing in an instant as I look up at the stars above with nothing but the sound of water spilling from the fall above. The throbbing in my shoulder pulsates to a soothing rhythm as the pain eases.

"Having fun?" a voice calls from ahead of me. Yaelor stands at the edge of the lagoon, her hands on her hips.

"Killian said the waters would help my shoulder. The waters, they're – they're incredible!"

"This is true, I do not think I have ever seen such clear waters." Her eyes lower from my face.

Mortified, I realise to what she alludes and my cheeks flush once again. Far too many times this has happened to me today. I quickly cover what modesty I have left with one of my hands.

"Relax, Laith, skin is skin. I do not understand why you are so precious." Yaelor unclips her top and lets it drop to the ground before lowering her pants. "I have already told you how my people see it."

I avert my eyes quickly but not quick enough. I see her tattooed skin in its entirety and my heart threatens to leave my chest, it beats that wildly.

The water splashes as she makes her way into the lagoon, and I turn to find her swimming towards me. I tread the water awkwardly, not knowing where to look or how to act, having never been in the company of a naked woman, let alone swimming with one.

"Yaelor, I need to apologise for before," I start. "I should not have taken my frustrations about Jordell out on you, and for that, I am sorry."

She continues her swim until she stops right in front of me, her face close to mine. Our breath caresses the surface of the water as her green eyes search my own.

"You paid the price for your words." She smiles and looks at my cheek. "When Barbaraqs have a quarrel, it ends there. They do not hold grudges. Neither do I."

She moves even closer, our breath touching, and as the blood rushes to my head and other areas, I feel as though I am going to pass out.

"As I said, I am sorry for how I behaved." My voice trembles as I speak. She is close enough to me that our bodies could touch at any moment in the water.

In this moment there is only me and her, our eyes remain fixed on one another. I have no idea what to do next.

"I do not understand why you are so nervous, are you offended?"

"No, no, that's really not the case," I answer even more awkwardly.

Yaelor looks down in the water before looking up and smiling at me, her eyebrow kinking up slightly.

Oh gods be damned, my lack of experience and control has got the better off me. I quickly turn away from her, embarrassed at myself. Her breath kisses the back of my neck and the water ripples as she moves in closer behind me, causing the hair on my neck to stand on edge.

"We are not disturbing you, are we?" Gillam's voice reaches us, and I spin quickly to see her and Vireo disrobing. They jump into the lagoon and splash around playfully, spraying water over one another before swimming in our direction.

How is it that everyone is comfortable in their own skin other than myself? "No, you're not." My voice almost breaks as I answer, and Yaelor smiles before swimming towards the others.

"This lagoon is something special, isn't it? We could not believe our luck when we found it. Well, it was Shadow that led us here," Vireo explains, treading the water with confidence.

"My shoulder does feels better now, so I'll probably go back," I reply, making my excuse to leave.

"Come, Laith, join us for a swim. Yaelor, are you staying?" Gillam asks.

Yaelor smiles and dives under the water, swimming

towards the waterfall. She moves gracefully as though from the ocean herself.

"I need to go apply the ointment that the healers gave me," I explain before swimming to the edge in haste. I climb out and grab hold of my clothes, quickly putting my cloth pants on. Vireo and Gillam are clearly entertained by my awkwardness as I head back to camp.

19

JORDELL

The flash of light that erupts in my eyes causes me to squint even though it is dark here. It takes me a moment to remember my situation as a state of confusion overcomes me.

"Where do you take me?" I ask, my voice hoarse and broken. My hands are bound tightly above me around a large branch that passes through the gap in my arms, and a strong fae male walks ahead of me, carrying the wood on his shoulder. I cannot see who is behind me but imagine another fae does the same from there. My head throbs where I was struck, and blood trickles down my face, dripping off the tip of my nose. My corrupted arm is in agony, my sleeve dropping to my elbow revealing the state it is in now. My skin is breaking where the thick black veins protrude, my arm reddening. It is as though my blood has been replaced with tar, and where the bindings dig into my skin it feels as though my wrists are clasped in red-hot irons. My feet drag behind me and I attempt to plant them, allowing me to walk, but I do not have the strength in my arms. The fae talk to one another in a tongue that I cannot decipher. Judging by the fact that I am still alive, I assume that they are intending to take me to whoever it is that leads them.

Panic overcomes me as I realise my satchel is not around my neck. I search franticly for it. Not so much for the elixirs but for the spellbook. I have not been parted from it since the day I was asked to transcribe it by Jareb. My surroundings are a mixture of blurred greens, my vision not fully returned. After a few minutes of searching, I see my satchel wrapped around a fae female who has one hand placed delicately on the top of it, the other firmly grasping a spear. Her eyes meet mine and she hisses at me in disapproval, causing me to look away in shame. There is something about those elixirs that they do not like, something that has offended them.

A shooting pain travels down my corrupted arm to my shoulders, and without any say in the matter a cry of pain leaves my lips. I quickly realise that the fae in front is taking great pleasure in jarring the wood so that my bindings press into my skin.

Large rows of homes created from the trees come into view, suspended in the air and with varying walkways, one of which the fae follow, taking us high into the trees, far higher than I thought possible. The varying tree huts are well crafted and constructed, their circular shapes swathed in canopies of trees that help blend them in to their natural backgrounds. As I am dragged over the suspended walkway, scores of fae adults, children, and adolescents, all of varying sizes and colours, stop to see the spectacle before them. I may not know their language, but I can see from their faces and the way they shield their younglings that they are afraid of me. They do not want their young to see me. Some escape to their perfectly crafted homes, some run down alternative walkways, while others stand their ground, fixing me with stares and growls of disapproval.

I pray for our journey to end as my arm screams with agony, the pain becoming unbearable. A bead of sweat traces down the congealed blood that decorates my face like war paint. It feels like we are moving for an age as we continue to traverse the walkways farther into where they live. It soon becomes apparent to me that this is not a village, it is a kingdom. An entire kingdom, an entire race of people living in the trees, that by my estimate equals the size of Askela, maybe even surpassing it. If not for my precarious position I would be in awe of it: columns of houses embedded into the largest trees I have ever seen, reaching above and below us. As I look down at the walkway, a funny feeling greets me as I am not familiar with these heights. I can see the ground far down below, but I cannot make out any details. I think this is the highest I have ever been, and a strange, sinking feeling greets me in the pit of my stomach. One that feels more like a warning than anything else.

The walkways all interconnect, some large and thick where multiple people can pass, some small and thin only big enough for one. The fae dart up and down them with ease as if walking a path on the ground. In this moment I am actually grateful for being bound and dragged, as at least this helps me feel grounded and less likely to fall over the sides. As we travel farther inside the kingdom, large birds fly past, sending gusts of air that blow my matted hair from my face. They are as big as horses, and to my surprise, a group of fae sits atop them in a way I would mount a steed. I dare not blink in case I miss anything. Insects the size of mice flutter uncontrollably in the tailwind of the large birds. Their wings are like bees but they are colourful like butterflies, large antennae circling from their heads. They buffet around for a moment before regaining their composure and fluttering off to sit on the base of a branch. A large fae woman rushes at them and shoes them away with a blanket, not appreciative of them taking a rest in front of her home.

The sections of wood on the walkways knock against the tops of my boots and I try again to raise myself to my feet, but I fail again. I am aching everywhere.

Ahead of us looms a large construct like nothing I have ever seen, like a castle made from wood. It sits at the highest point of the trees, looking out across the rest of the fae kingdom. I take a deep inhale of breath as my eyes dart around the castle, unable to comprehend the workmanship and the skill to craft such a thing. Large turret towers look as though they have been carved from wood, and what I think are stones turn out to be detailed intricate carvings etched into the wall. An arch bows above the wall that connects the two turret towers, with perches protruding from the front. Sitting atop the perch are the riders, complete with birds standing guard.

What an interesting concept, having bird riders be the first line of defence against any attackers. I count five all standing guard, the birds that the fae ride upon keeping a beady eye on things that are going on below. One of them stands tall and spreads out its wings, demonstrating an impressive wingspan. Another swoops down from the top of the perch and lands in front of us, blocking our path. This one looks like a giant crow, its feathers as black as the night. It too spreads out its wings as if telling my captors to stop. They do, and the fae sporting me bow their heads to the rider.

The leader of our group exchanges words with the rider, who casts me a look of disgust. Then she pulls on the harness of her bird, and it propels itself upwards with tremendous force, the gust of air it generates taking me by surprise as it presses against me. The bird and its rider disappear over the top of the castle walls, and our party continues the ascent to the highest point of the kingdom to stand before the castle gates. They stand tall, about thirty feet high, made of wood and wrapped with vines for reinforcement. The wood is finely crafted and sculpted into position, with the tips of the gates intertwined as though the wood still lives as it binds itself into shape.

There is a mechanical noise as the gate lowers down in front of us like a drawbridge. The last of the walkway rocks as it slams into the ground, allowing us entry.

Beyond the gates, two riders stand in the centre of a large open space. Between them stands a fae woman whose skin is as pale as snow, almost as if it has a blueish tinge to it. Her pointed ears are pierced with delicate chains that flow from the top to the bottom of her lobes. A thin crown pins her dark hair in place atop her head, and the rest flows down her shoulder freely.

Suddenly my mouth feels dry. I am in the company of fae royalty.

Her long, elegant gown flows gracefully to the ground, covering her feet. Her arms are bare, revealing the same tree-like tattoos that the other fae have. But unlike the others', hers shine as if the ink itself is crafted from silver. Her beauty mesmerises me, and I find myself drawn to the natural aura that she radiates.

We stand in a pristine courtyard where finely polished stone graces the floor as though it has just been laid, untainted or scuffed from heavy feet. Around us, wildflowers have been allowed to grow over seats and railings that only serves to further amplify the beauty of this kingdom. Behind this mysterious fae queen I can see a fountain with the most elegant of statues in the centre. What looks like three fae maidens are busy scooping up water into buckets which they then disappear from view with.

The party stops in front of her, and suddenly I feel far heavier than before. As my back arches, the pressure becomes worse, and I drag my feet so I can at least hold myself up in a standing position. My arms remain suspended in the air as I stand to attention, paraded in front of the fae woman.

The group leader speaks loudly and clearly, announcing why it is they are here, and I am taken aback by this strangely human formality. The fae that carries my satchel moves forward, removing it from over her neck and passing it to this fae queen. The queen reaches in and takes out the spellbook, tracing her fingers over its surface before sniffing the pages deeply. Next, she is handed the elixirs, and her perplexed expression turns into one of utter confusion and then anger.

The queen glides across the floor towards me with surprising speed as if walking on air, almost spirit-esque. Her face changes from a picture of beauty to one of sharpened teeth and rage.

My heart drums even louder as her snarling face draws far closer to mine than I would have liked.

"*Fredu, radia trevortee jeru,*" she says, slowly and concisely. I have no clue to the words she speaks, just as with the others. She turns and glowers at the leader of this group before meeting my gaze again. Her eyes could have been carved from diamonds, and her skin seems to sparkle, though maybe it's a trick of the light. Her snarling expression tells me that she is far more dangerous than her beautiful, jewel-like appearance suggests.

She opens her mouth again, this time speaking words that I understand clearly. "Tell me, wizard, what have you done with Aruya?" She pulls a curved knife from the back of her belt and quickly presses this against my neck. I feel the sting of the blade against my skin as my nerves start to get the better of me. This is as close to death as I have ever felt, the afterlife threatening to greet me at any moment.

"Tell me what you have done with my daughter!"

20

LAITH

My mind cycles between Jordell, Orjan, and Yaelor, and I cannot sleep. Even the healer's remedy fails to soothe me, and the rough wool sheet scratches uncomfortably against my skin. What's more, it would appear an owl has taken up residence far closer to my hut than I would like.

One final hoot tips me over the edge.

"Fuck!" I sit bolt upright, kicking off my quilt with frustration. It slides to the floor with a thud.

There is nothing worse than desperately wanting to draw on sleep but being unable to. Maybe a walk will help.

Itchy with restlessness, I drag myself out of bed and redress myself, my pants still slightly damp from when I made my escape from the lagoon.

I exit my hut and take in a deep breath of air, savouring the fresh pine smell that the forest brings. There are no signs of anyone within the camp itself, save for someone sitting by an open fire in the centre where Killian made his soup earlier.

"At least I am not the only one who can't sleep," I tell

myself before navigating the walkway to the lower levels. I walk as quietly as I can, but the planks creak under my weight, the noise amplified by the silence of the night.

When I reach the floor, I find myself grounded by the feeling of solid footing, and I make my way over to the figure by the fire.

Gillam sits there, the hood of her red cloak drawn over her head as she stokes the fire with a metal skewer. Her eyes are vacant, and she does not notice me as I approach.

"Mind if I join you?" I whisper.

Gillam startles back and I worry for a moment that she is about to strike me with the skewer that she holds.

"Shit," she curses, "you startled me!" She throws on an additional log, and the fire crackles, emitting a slow hiss as the sap inside starts to boil. "Why are you sneaking around at this time, Laith?"

I am surprised at her jumpiness; the Gillam I know is a master of the shadows. Maybe her time here has lessened her skills.

"Sorry." I take a seat beside her. "I couldn't sleep. You?"

"I have dreams. Well, nightmares," she says, the glow of the flames mirrored in her dark eyes.

"What about? That is, if you don't mind me asking?"

Gillam huffs and stokes the fire again, as though she is conflicted in whether or not she wants to share her worries with me.

"Jordell always told me that if something is on your mind, it is better sharing it with someone, that way the burden we carry is easier to manage," I say, casting Gillam a smile.

She returns a slight smile, half her face cased in the shadows of her hood. "He is a wise man, that mage of ours."

"He prefers 'wizard'. He doesn't like being called a mage. He doesn't want to be associated with the darker magic that

Morgana brings to the battlefield," I explain. "So, what is it that troubles your dreams so much that you would rather sit alone in the dead of night?"

"Lek." She sighs deeply, as though the words she forms weigh heavy enough on their own. "That bastard, and what he did to us, what he did to me. Each night I live through the battle in Askela and my duel against him." She pauses, searching for words. "Being kicked from the upper ledge and falling to my fate. He nearly killed me, he fucking broke me. For months afterwards I had to learn how to walk again, dependent on others to clothe me, feed me, bathe me. Relying entirely on others to survive. In those darkened days, I often thought that if I was able to move freely, I would have gladly ended it. But I was too weak, I wasn't even able to act on my wishes. And for what? So he could take our land and coin and claim it as his own? We had been through so much together. I would have gladly died for him on the battlefield." She leans forward and grabs another small log, placing it delicately into the flames. Her tears fall from her face, sizzling in an instant as they clash with the white-hot embers.

To see Gillam so vulnerable pulls at my heart and it breaks for the pain she has been through since Jordell and I left this camp. She has been on a journey that has moulded her, shaped her, and this is what remains. Somehow through the ashes, she has risen up.

"I think you do not give yourself credit for the strength you have shown in your darkest moments, Gillam. Many would have given up, many would not have tried. But you did."

Gillam places her knuckles together in front of her and cracks them.

"What was that?" I ask.

She smiles and brings up a hand quickly to wipe away the stream of tears that runs down her face. "Something I used to do when I was at my weakest, most desperate. When I could not move, I did it to help me focus, I did it to centre me in this world. It serves two purposes. One, that I will be okay." She pauses again, wiping another tear from her face. "And two, that Lek will pay for the things he has done. Not just to me but to the people of Askela under the rule of Morgana."

We would be forgiven in this moment for thinking we were the only people in camp, a quiet air surrounding us as we talk with one another. A wild-looking man walks past, his hair thick and long, his beard engulfing his face only revealing two tired eyes. He causes me to jump and offers me a nod and a smile, no doubt on his way to set up watch somewhere.

"If you breathe a word of this, I will kill you in your sleep." Gillam smiles, but there is a seriousness in her face that I would not want to test.

"That's the Gillam I know."

Gillam fetches both her hands up to her face this time and washes away what tears remain, her cheeks blotched. "That is enough about my plight. What of yours?"

"It can wait, it doesn't matter."

"Bah," she snorts, "remember those wise words of Jordell's you just imparted a short time ago?"

Gillam has a point. I would be a hypocrite for letting her spill her soul to me but then not offer my own thoughts. I take a deep breath and find the words hard to form in my head. "Jordell, I hate how I left things."

"We spoke about this earlier, did we not?"

"Yes. It's not just Jordell, there are other things too. This quest, for example, and where it ends. Either way, Jordell is adamant that a Great War is coming, and I need to make sure I am in a position to protect those who I care about most."

"You mean Jordell," Gillam says shortly.

"No, not just Jordell. I care about here, I care about Vireo.

You. I couldn't bear it if anything happened to any of you. It does not bear thinking about, but I fear for how I would cope with such a loss."

"You truly love him, don't you?"

"As a son would his father." It is the first time I have admitted such outside of my own thoughts.

"What about Yaelor?" Gillam asks, looking me deep in my eyes. Her eyes catch the light of the fire, causing them to almost glow in the dark like that of a cat's. "You seemed cosy earlier today." Gillam turns slightly, her speech less confident and more awkward, and I can't tell if she teases me or something else.

"I have not known her long. She is a strong woman, what she has been through to be here with us today. She carries steel in her heart. The only other person I have seen that strong, or that confident, is you." A silence hangs in the air. Gillam turns her head away from me to stare into the fire.

"Then there is Orjan."

"Orjan?" Gillam looks confused by my words. This is a name she will not have heard for some time, but one she will recognise nonetheless. It was her and Lek who gave him the beating that led to him abandoning me as his squire. That led me to this moment, sitting by Gillam in front of a roaring fire in the middle of the night.

"We hear he is a cursed man, one who bears the skin of a lizard, and that he fights alongside Morgana." Saying it out loud feels as though I spray hot ash from my lips.

"I see, and you need to know if this is true?"

"I need to ride to Eltera and see for myself."

"You cannot go traipsing into the kingdom like that. We are all wanted by the Crown, whether the king is alive or not. If you are captured, you will be tortured and killed." Gillam's expression turns to one of concern. She rests her hands on top of mine. "You cannot risk your life with such brash decisions. Let me send a messenger on your behalf. If it is Orjan, maybe we can find a way to meet him away from Eltera."

"You would do that for me?" I am surprised at the tenderness with which she holds my hand and the kindness she shows.

"Of course I would, Laith. I have always been fond of you. Let me share these burdens with you. Let me help." She leans into me and my heart races for what I think is about to come. She kisses me on my cheek, her soft, warm lips pressing against my skin, and I feel as though my face is about to implode.

Feeling awkward, I keep my vision fixed on the fire. There is a silence between us, my heart racing at the sudden affection Gillam has displayed. It has caught me off guard, like taking a joust to the chest from a knight on a galloping steed.

"I, er . . ." I curse myself for being such a bumbling fool. Why can I not display the levels of confidence that Vireo does?

"Come, the hour is late. Our burdens shared will hopefully allow us to rest." Gillam does not wait for me to answer before getting to her feet. "I will send a messenger in the morning to Eltera." There is a coldness to her words that tells me my reaction is not what she was hoping for. How I am an idiot. She makes her leave without another word, leaving me alone with the crackling fire.

I can't help but feel that when I return to my bed, I will find it even harder to sleep now.

21

JORDELL

"Lord Myrion Sand is dead, his wine poisoned while dining with his wife. We cannot be sure who is responsible but I fear that Lady Morgana had something to do with his death. She is dangerous and I am sure she seeks to ascend the throne herself. This would not be good for the Great Temple, she has shown herself to be our enemy long before she rose to power."

DORIAN FIRO, Scholar to The Great Temple in Eltera, 255 KR

"WHERE IS MY DAUGHTER!" the fae woman hisses in my ear. She holds the dagger tightly against my throat, to the point where I find myself holding my breath, not wanting to risk contact with the blade.

"I do not know," I answer, my voice rasping and constrained.

"LIAR!" she cries as she continues to press the dagger

against my skin. "Now tell me what this is and why it carries the essence of Aruya?"

"I don't know!" I repeat. "All I can offer is the circumstances that we came to be in possession of that elixir."

There is anger and hatred in the fae's eyes, one that draws on pain and worry.

"I was in the nearby woodlands, between the Forest of Opiya and Eltera," I tell her carefully. "Our party was making our way here when we crossed paths with some guards who sought to capture us. One of them drank this elixir, and it changed them, enraged them. The elixir enabled him to cast storm magic."

"Silence," the fae demands. "I know your race, I know all too well the lies and tales that humans will spin to achieve their own agenda."

"I am telling you the truth. Please, I seek only to find answers to the questions that I myself have. I carry magic in me, I bear the markings of a spellcaster. See for yourself." I direct her gaze to my arm which is still bound above me. The fae woman glances up at my corrupted wound. "Except I fear that I may have overused my magic of late, the burden of which my body can no longer carry."

"Your body is breaking due to the strain of magic, a sign that those not born of the forest do not understand the powers that you wield. The first elves were the same, born from a relationship between fae and humans."

"I only aim to help others in need. I do not know what has happened to your daughter but if you will allow it, I would help you get the answers that you seek."

The fae paces away from me before turning, her eyes clenched tightly shut as she roars out in anger. She swings the blade towards me and I close my eyes, embracing the impending strike that will surely end me. I pray quickly to the gods that Laith and the others will remain safe.

There is a thud and I find myself slamming to the ground like dead weight. As my arms land in front of me, I realise my bindings have been cut. A shooting pain travels up my corrupted arm in waves of pulsating agony as my blood begins to recirculate.

"Thank you," I manage to muster through the pain, although I struggle to bring myself to my feet, having been dragged all the way here. Remaining on the floor, I take some deep gasps of air as I breathe in a sigh of relief.

"Fool me, spellcaster, and I will see to it that not only your life ends, but all of those that are camped on the outskirts of our forest. The gods may will them to be here, but you will meet the full wrath of a queen if you cross me." She stands in front of me, her curved blade still pointed in my direction.

"Please, my name is Jordell. In my lands I am known as a mage – a wizard. I only cast magic that will help or heal others," I explain, my arms trembling as I force myself into an upright position. With one last rugged heave, I manage to get myself standing upright. The queen is at least a foot taller than me.

She nods, as if accepting my words. "My daughter's magic is somehow in this." The queen raises the blackened elixir in front of her face. "My daughter was taken at the outer edges of the forest. I told her not to go but with faerie wells being raided, she insisted on going to help and find out more information. When she did not return, our greatest fears were realised. Our kind is being taken away from the forest. Our scouts have fed back that they are being kept in one of your fortresses. The one called Askela."

"Morgana," I breathe. "She is the one responsible for the

taking of your people. I have been in conflict with her myself for years past."

"That does not answer my question of how my daughter's essence has come to be in this potion that you have brought me." She sniffs it again as though smelling the essence reminds her of her daughter, but then her face changes to one of fear. "I must know what has happened, I must find out what this Morgana has done."

I look around at the vast kingdom at her disposal, the bird riders she has, the number of warriors she must command. "If you know where they take your people, why do you not storm Askela and take them back?" I ask.

"We cannot leave this place. Our magic is tied to this forest, to the trees. It is our life source, our essence. To leave would render us weakened and lead us to certain death. I cannot threaten the existence of my race no matter how strong the temptation to save the lives of a few. No matter what the price is to myself."

"Let me help you. Let me and my friends travel to Askela in your stead. All I ask in return is that no more blood is shed of my friends' camp. I would also ask for your help or guidance on something I am searching for."

The queen thinks on this for a moment "If you bring my daughter back, I will remove that corruption from your arm."

"This corruption, can it happen to those injured by your magic?"

"Yes," she says, slowly, untrusting eyes raking over my skin. "Corruption can taint any person touched by magic, whether casting it or being hit by it. If the corruption travels far enough through the veins, it will likely bring about their end."

My fears are confirmed, then. Laith's life is in danger as well, should the corruption that seeps into him continue to grow. My search for the sword must wait. For now, I must help Laith, and quickly. If I can help return her people, there is still a chance that he can survive his wound. Then we will not only have gained the fae as an ally, but I will be able to rid us both from the corruption.

"Your majesty, I will do what I can to help you."

"My name is Zariah. If you bring back my people, I will owe you a great debt. There is something different about you, Jordell. You do not seem like the other humans that I have met before you. They prowl this kingdom in search of treasures and wealth, whereas I believe you to be speaking the truth. Why else would the healing magic you possess course through your veins? It is as the gods will it."

Zariah looks up towards the tops of the trees that stretch high as though they attempt to reach the gods themselves. She raises her hand gently in the air as spores from the trees land on her, and she examines it before absorbing them into her skin. I can't help but feel that she draws her own magic this way, like a form of osmosis. It is a spectacle to behold.

"You hold a rare magic indeed, but your human form is too fragile to maintain it. The elves, on the other hand, knew their limitations and would not allow their magic to break them. That said, if you carry magic then you are a descendant of this forest, as elves were formed of a bond between fae and humans. Your kind were formed from the bonding between humans and elves. In each descendant, the magic is a diluted version of our own power, unable to draw on the energy of the Great Tree, instead drawing on the power within your own life force."

I think I understand to what she is alluding, although my mind aches, part from the information Zariah has imparted on me, part from the blow to the head I have taken. I have so many questions that I want to ask but the most pressing matter is that of gaining Queen Zariah's trust. Of finding where the fae are being kept in Askela and returning them to her.

"Please hold onto my affects until I return, and mark my words, I will return. There is a Great War coming to Levanthria and we need to be prepared as best as we can."

"I care not for the wars that you people wage upon yourselves. I care only for my people and my daughter. Beware of the price you will pay if you do not return with Aruya." With this, the queen turns to make her leave, flicking her hand above her shoulder. "See our guest is returned to where you found him."

22

LAITH

With a thump, the axe that I wield cuts through the wood. I stack the newly chopped log and go again. It is a hot, humid day and my shirt sticks to me like the unwanted advances of a hag. The waters from the lagoon and the ointment I have been applying have done their job and although my shoulder still aches, it feels much stronger than it did. That said, the stinging around the blackened edges of the wound itself continues, and my frayed skin remains damaged despite the healers ointments and creams. The scarring I assume will be beyond healing. When I inspected it closely, I swear the black burns were stretching out in a vein like formation across my shoulder. The healers have assured me that in time it should heal, although they have never seen anything like this before, which doesn't give me the greatest reassurance. Even so, there are more important things going on at the moment, which push the lingering effects of the magic-inflicted wound to the back of my mind. It has been two further days since Gillam sent a messenger in search of

Orjan. I have waited in bated anticipation for word back from him.

For now, I have opted to help with chores around camp. The trees that are felled are ones that have been planted within the camp's perimeters. Vireo has explained we must not fell the trees outside of camp. Even though they grow at an accelerated rate, the camp still requires the occasional party to journey to the nearby woodlands outside of the forest in order to cultivate wood for fires and building.

Yaelor soon joins me in my task, and she proves to be far better than I at chopping wood. She is not immune to the heat of the day, though, and sweat flows over her body. She grunts loudly as she cleaves a small log in two with one swing of her axe, then she slams her axe into the ground before picking up the two pieces and placing them onto the pile besides us.

Whilst she does this, I place a slightly larger log with its side up so the rings of the felled tree face me. It is about the size of a dinner plate, so I should be able to manage it.

Spurred on by how easily Yaelor cut through her log, I raise my axe above my head and bring it down with as much force as I can muster. My axe bounces off and I hear Yaelor snigger behind me. I bring my axe down a second time, but still the log does not break. On the third attempt it does, which brings me a strange sense of satisfaction despite needing repeated attempts.

"You are a strong man. Maybe one day you will be a good Barbaraq," she laughs, placing a log which was bigger than mine. She raises her axe high above her, her wet muscles rippling in the light. I am in awe at the strength that she carries. With a crash, she slams the axe down and it bounces off, and this time I cannot help but muster a snigger. It only serves to spur her on and after a slight adjustment of her frame, she brings the axe down even harder. Wood splinters everywhere as the log is cleaved in two. Yaelor rest her axe on her shoulder and offers me a wry smile.

"Okay, you win," I laugh, "but remember I am still not recovered from my injury."

She smiles back at me, which brings me a warmth that I find comforting. "You are forgetting that I had one foot in the afterlife when our paths first crossed."

That much is true. As much as my shoulder has given me hell since we crossed paths with the would-be mage, Yaelor was in a far worse state when we met her.

"Do you think this is enough?" I ask, casting my eyes proudly over the pile of chopped wood. My body aches from the chore, but I feel stronger for it, a strange sense of euphoria riding my body in the aftermath of the work. I pick up my water bottle and offer it to Yaelor first, but she shakes her head so I take a large gulp instead. It is refreshingly crisp and cool, and with being so hot, I pour the rest of the water over my head before ruffling my hair. It does as intended, cooling me to my core. If I were much warmer, steam would surely emit from my pores.

I catch Yaelor looking, but she does not seem ashamed. Her confidence is like nothing I have ever experienced. I shake my bottle and see there is a small bit left in the bottom, so I pour the last of the contents into my mouth.

"You will make a good mate one day," she says.

I can't hold the water and it sprays out in front of me. She laughs to herself before collecting some of the wood. "Come, let's take this back to camp."

I want the ground to swallow me whole. What does she mean, one day?

Gillam has kept herself away from me following my awkward response to her kiss by the campfire, and I do not blame her. I have spent much of my time completing tasks to aid the camp with the help of Yaelor.

"One day, Laith, you will figure out what exactly being a man is."

I sigh to myself as I lift two logs and carry them back towards the camp.

It takes us into the later part of the day by the time we have carried the wood back to the wood stores. If I thought my arms and back ached earlier, it pales in comparison to what I experience now. Our task now complete, I plan on ending my day with a trip to the lagoon and a dip in those waters. After Killian's tale and the way my shoulder is feeling, I share his and the others conviction that the waters contain healing properties. Raising my hand, I place it on the wound to find it feeling hot to the touch, as though an infection takes hold, even though the healers continue to insist the infection has passed.

As I exit the wood stores, I make to head straight to the lagoon, hoping it is quiet so I can bathe in peace.

"Ah, Laith I was just looking for you." Vireo's voice causes me to spin on the spot to face him, his grin as wide as his face. "Looks as though you have had a busy day chopping wood." I look down on myself and my clothes are filled with dirt and are damp with my sweat, my shirt sticking to my skin.

"I was just about to go for a swim and clean myself up," I explain.

"Before you do, I was hoping that you and Yaelor may like to spar with Gillam and I? It would be nice to see where your sword skills are up to after all this time."

I don't even hide the fact that my eyes roll. My body aches and I am tired beyond belief following our day's labour. Now he asks me to spar.

"I never miss the chance to spar against an equal or

someone stronger. This is how we grow," Yaelor announces with pride as she exits the wood store.

"I knew I liked you." Vireo grins. "Follow me." Vireo looks as though he has been gifted a present. The last thing I want to do now is spar. If only I could share the same enthusiasm as Yaelor who follows Vireo at pace like an over-excited pup.

When we reach the camp, Gillam waits by a weapons rack, wearing her more familiar dark leathers, her hair scraped back tightly and tied. She makes fleeting eye contact with me before picking up her daggers from the rack.

"Here we are." Vireo grabs two swords and passes one to me. It is weighted, but I am able to balance it okay. It is always strange sparring with a blade you are not familiar with, but mine remains with one of the smiths who is carrying out repair work.

Yaelor grins wildly as she pores over the weapons as if inspecting ancient treasures. "Now these are the kind of weapons of my people," she says as she picks up two hatchets and holds them low by her sides.

"Shall we?" Gillam asks, stony faced.

"Right, let's see how you have grown over these years, boy." Vireo raises his sword and slides it up and down mine whilst casting me a grin. "Brings back old memories."

"That it does." I press my sword against him to flex my strength and show him I am no longer the boy he seems to think I am.

"That's the spirit. Now remember, no kill shots. This is a spar, after all." He winks at me.

I lunge forward to strike first.

Vireo is quick to this and as he steps back, he parries my blow. I push forward and strike a second time, then a third. Each blow Vireo blocks as I aim to show him just how strong I have become. In truth, I have waited a long time for this moment. My memory serves me flashes of the time he put me on my arse. I won't let that happen again.

"My, my, you are stronger," Vireo teases. He adapts his stance and points his sword towards me, stretching out his free hand behind him as if he is some sort of scorpion. Gripping my blade tightly, I swipe rashly, but he knocks my sword to the side before spinning towards me in a blur. Before I can do anything, he is behind me and slaps me on the arse with the blunt side of his sword.

"Come on, boy, that was too easy," he taunts.

"It's not like I've been chopping wood all day, Vireo," I snap, irked by his words. I take a few steps from him and circle to face him once more, swinging my sword in a spiral by rotating my wrist.

Vireo copies me, beckoning me to try and strike him again. "Try to not make it so easy this time. I said I wanted to spar!"

I know his game. He seeks to goad me into acting brashly and letting my guard down. A crowd of people forms around us, curious about the spectacle.

"Vireo ain't going to lose this one," a large man states, his voice deep and low.

"Nah, the boy's got youth on his side," another smaller man counters.

Boy. The word stews in the back of my head like a mould-encrusted steak. What is it with everyone around here that insists on calling me boy? Why do they not acknowledge my age? I step forward and strike again, this time from the side. Vireo knocks my sword back with ease.

"The boy is too inexperienced." The large man's commentary is not helping.

I quickly swing again, this time even wilder than before, but Vireo simply jumps back away from me, not even needing to dodge the blow. My arms burn with tiredness, an ache nestling deep in my shoulder, my tensed muscles on the verge of cramping at any moment. I pause, panting for breath.

Vireo grins from ear to ear, cocksure and barely winded.

"I thought you said you had been training."

My ears and cheeks burn with a flash of heat as people in the crowd laugh at my expense.

"Again!" Vireo demands.

I hold my ground, thinking about my next move. "No," I call back with defiance, "you strike first this time."

"That's the spirit, there's the spark I know you have. I thought you would never bloody ask!" He rushes at me far faster than I expect, and I've barely had time to adapt my defensive stance when he is upon me. He drags his sword out wide, and I shift my weight onto my left foot to defend to my right, gripping the hilt of my blade so tightly that I fear my knuckles may pop from their joints.

Before my steel can meet his, he feigns his strike. With his free hand he brings his open palm across my face. In that moment I would have rather taken a fist.

A fire burns within me from the humiliation, and I wish for nothing more than to put him on his smug arse. As he stands grinning at me like the cat who got the cream, I feint my own blow quickly and offer a full boot to his stomach. It connects, and I hear the rasp of air leave his lungs. Our blades crash over and over as we begin combat in earnest now, and I show him just what I am capable of with my blade. For a few moments we are evenly matched, no person getting the upper hand, and my confidence starts to grow –

My foot slides over mud, causing me to lose my footing and jarring my back in the process. Before I know it, I am greeted with the view of the canopy of trees above me. Vireo points his blade towards my chest.

"Do you yield?" he asks.

"I yield."

Vireo beams down at me and offers me a hand, heaving me to my feet. My pride is bruised more than anything.

"I think I put up a better fight when I was younger," I say, brushing the dirt from the back of my pants.

"You were trying to kill me back then."

"Who says I wasn't now?"

Vireo pauses for a moment before bursting into laughter and offering me his hand to shake, which I accept.

"You still have much to learn. Keep a cool head and you will do fine in battle. Jordell tells me how accomplished you are with a blade. It was a simple slip that helped me best you."

That, and letting his words get to me. Perhaps if I showed the same composure as Vireo, it would be him wiping the muck from his clothes.

Loud grunts and groans interrupt us, and my attention is jarred by Yaelor and Gillam who continue their sparring. They move with ferocious speed, attacking with grit and gusto, and I can't help but feel as though there is tension in the air, thick enough for me to notice it. The two of them connect their weapons and press against one another, teeth bared, muscles taut with tension.

Gillam says something to Yaelor but I am not close enough to hear her words. The people watching who stand closer shake their heads in disapproval.

Whatever it is seems to ignite a fire within Yaelor. She forces Gillam's arms back before slamming her head into her nose. Gillam's face explodes with crimson, and she stumbles backwards. She repositions herself, ready to continue regardless.

Yaelor pants, sweat coursing down her face and body. She stares at Gillam, raising her hatchets in the air. She then tosses them to the ground and raises her hands.

"I will never be accepted by your people," she says, not in anger, but in pain. She is hurting. She turns to leave, Gillam still snarling.

"What in the blazes was that about?" Given the scolding I had from Gillam just a few days ago in defence of Yaelor, I am surprised at the venom she now shows towards her. I follow Yaelor to check she is okay; I know what it is to be disheartened, lonely.

A vice-like grip around my arm stops me. "I would let the dust settle first," Vireo warns. "Best not get in the way of two women marking their territory."

I am confused by his words, but there is no time to ask him his meaning; something rustles in the trees nearby. I clutch my blade, readying myself for an ogre to emerge from the forest, or worse.

No beast appears, however, but rather a dishevelled-looking Jordell. His face is full of dirt, his greying beard matted, his hair ruffled and unkept. He looks as though he has been sleeping in the wild and woken in a zarobi nest.

"Jordell!" I exclaim, tossing my blade to the side and embracing him tightly, my worries slipping away in an instant. A wave of emotion overcomes me that I am not expecting, catching me off guard harder than Vireo's slap.

He is alive, he is here.

23

JORDELL

"As Levanthria becomes accustomed to the more familiar use of magic, there has been a growing rumour about a once secret and hidden group of mages growing in confidence across the land."

VALERAN BUETA, *Scribe to The Great Temple, 254 KR*

"You want us to do *what*?" Vireo exclaims, his voice cracked and frustrated. "Jordell, this is madness. These creatures have killed our people and now you ask us to rescue their kin?"

Vireo's reaction is exactly what I expected.

We stand around the main fire in the centre of camp, its flames kissing the air, Vireo, Killian, Gillam, Laith and Yaelor deep in heated conversation.

"Please listen, Vireo. I understand your reluctance to lend your aid to this task. Without your support, however, I feel our chances of this raid being a success are far slimmer." In truth, it will take more than the gods' favour for us to be able to pull this off. The last time I set foot in Askela was when we did battle inside the castle gates, when I shared Morgana's vision.

"I am a better man than I was, Jordell. But what you ask, it is too much." Vireo's pacing threatens to dig the deepest of trenches in the soil.

Gillam sits by the fire, a bloodied cloth held to her face. "Vireo, I feel as conflicted about this as you. But it sounds like Jordell brings an olive branch from the fae. We need to think about this camp, our people. This could end our conflict, this could help us expand our boundaries."

"Are the tunnels still usable?" Laith asks. "That would grant us access close to the castle gates."

I had no doubt that Laith would be on side. I know he would follow me into battle anywhere, no matter the odds.

Killian strokes his thick beard with his hand. "Aye, the tunnels are still accessible as far as I know, but we have been using them less and less as Codrin has made it increasingly difficult to get supplies inside the kingdom."

"Even if I did agree to this insanity, the guards will be on high alert," Vireo protests. "With the king's death, Morgana will not want an uprising. It is only a matter of time before she stakes a claim to the throne."

"How, though?" Laith asks. "She is not noble born. Surely the likes of yourself has a better claim to the throne than she does. You are from nobility."

"That I am, but after I killed Jareb, King Athos granted stewardship to Morgana. He has no heir and Jareb was the last of his bloodline. As Jareb had no children, it means their lineage has died, too. All that would remain would be for Morgana to stake her claim as steward."

Vireo is right in what he says; the situation for Levanthria is unprecedented.

"There has never been a queen rule Levanthria, and I'll be damned if she's the first," Gillam spits.

She has a point in what she says. I could think of a hundred women that would suit the throne better than her.

"Would she not need the backing of the lords of the lands?" Laith asks, almost out of desperation to find a way to untangle all of this.

"Would you want to oppose or challenge Morgana?" Killian demands.

Laith has a look in his eye that I am all too familiar with as he nods, confirming that he would.

"You're the wrong person to ask," Killian counters. "Anyone in this camp has the balls to challenge her. Or the stupidity. Unfortunately, we are not high-ranking lords and as such we have no say on who ascends the throne. No one with any land or riches would be foolish enough to challenge her. She is too powerful. To do so would be a death sentence."

"All this does not deter from what you ask of us, Jordell." Vireo brings the group back to focus, which I am grateful for.

"The fae are not bad people, they are just not trusting of man –"

"Try explaining they are not bad to Hera, Cruwis, and Yera's families," Vireo snaps.

"What I ask of you will surely build these bridges and prevent further bloodshed. This is the right path, Vireo. If you had seen their kingdom, if you had seen the craftsmanship, the knowledge that they possess. If they were your ally and not your enemy . . . Your people would be safe, from the creatures of the forest and from those that would put our heads on a pike in Levanthria."

Vireo and the others don't know about the corruption that seeps through my body, and I plan to keep it that way. I need them to make this decision based on practicalities alone, not for the cure that could rid me of this affliction and save Laith's life.

"When I joined the Great Temple, I swore an oath to aid and protect those unable to do so themselves," I explain.

"I care not for the Great Temple, Jordell. If your gods existed then would all this suffering across Levanthria be happening? Would you be needing to risk your life so often to prevent a Great War that has not even graced us yet?" Spit leaves Vireo's mouth as he speaks, his face red.

"I will do what I must, old friend. I will do what I can to aid the fae. Because it is the right thing to do. If a consequence of that is bringing peace for you and your camp, it is a risk I am happy to take." My voice is calm yet determined. I know in my mind what I must do, and no amount of dialogue will change that. "I will not force anyone to join me on this endeavour. After all, you are right: it is madness." I cast Vireo a smile as I use his own words against him.

"I am in," Laith says immediately.

Gillam picks up her daggers from her side and stands up as though ready to lead the assault. "I can only hope our paths cross with Lek's. I will not hide in the shadows when I end his miserable existence. I want him to look right into my eyes when I send him to the afterlife."

"You have my axe, too," Killian adds.

Vireo casts his eyes upon us one by one, exasperated. He sighs. "Well, I can't let you all go into Askela on your own."

I smile at him, happy that he has decided to join us. Killian fetches a stick and starts etching a rough outline of Askela in the dirt by the campfire.

Before I know it, the dead of night catches up with us, a cold chill sitting damply within the trees. My breath hangs in the air like a steamed drink as I check the last of my wares. I tend to one of the horses to make sure everything is ready before we make our journey.

The large grey steed I will be riding has a plaited mane and tail, something I believe the children of the camp like to do to pass the time. It turns its head to me as I pat it on the neck, its warm breath giving my iced cheeks a brief reprieve. I open up my hand to reveal a large, green apple, which the steed gratefully accepts, chomping down on it.

"Are you sure of this plan?"

The words cause me to jump and my horse pulls its head away as Laith stands beside me. He wears his cloak, ready to set off on the journey.

"How is your shoulder?" I ask.

Laith rotates it a few times. "As good as it will get for the time being."

"Then I have every faith in this plan working." I smile, patting him on the back before climbing onto my horse. "Are the others ready?"

"We are," Vireo answers. He walks towards me wearing his dark emerald-green cloak, closely followed by Gillam, Killian, and Yaelor. Each of them appears ready for combat, each one willing to sacrifice their own safety in order to save members of the fae that, until a couple of days ago, I did not know existed.

They each get on a horse, and we stand side by side on the outer edges of the camp.

"We need to make haste if we are to keep the darkness on our side," I say.

Vireo pulls his hood up over his head and the others follow.

Then we begin to ride towards whatever fate awaits us in Askela.

24

LAITH

"We are here." Killian's hushed words bring us to a halt as we approach the end of the tunnels, deep inside Askela. This is a kingdom I have not been to in a long time, not since the days of being a runner for Vireo, bringing much-needed coin into the city to help those who needed it most.

The tunnels are in a bad state. The ground is sodden, the air damp and musky with nothing but torchlight to guide us. If some much-needed repair work is not completed soon on the braces that prevent the soil from collapsing, this tunnel will likely cease to be of use.

Killian stands at the front, me at the rear. He climbs a rope ladder to the ceiling where he presses the trap door that leads to his old tavern. The squeak of wood on wood tells me the trap door has swollen due to the damp.

Killian uses his shoulder and hammers into the trap door once more, and this time it opens. The noise echoes down the tunnel where we stand, raising my paranoia of guards hearing us. Killian disappears, and the others begin their ascent one by one.

The ladder seems far smaller than the last time I was here. I grip one of the rungs tightly before climbing up and poking my head through the trap door. When I exit, I am greeted by further damp, the sound of dripping water as it leaks through the ceiling and down the walls of the tavern.

"Extinguish the torches," Vireo hisses, "we don't want to draw unnecessary attention to ourselves."

We do as he asks, the smoke from the burning oil granting me a brief reprieve from the mouldy stench that the tavern gifts us.

Around us, the building is in a state of disrepair, tables broken and overturned, glasses smashed. Charred remains of books litter the fireplace, used by people desperate to stay warm.

"For the road?" Killian lifts a bottle of whisky from behind the bar. "This is as old a whisky as there is in all of Levanthria. I have kept it hidden for a special occasion. Given we are walking into a bear pit, I refuse to do so without tasting its crispness one last time." He raises the bottle back and takes a gulp, gasping loudly in appreciation.

Vireo accepts this with a grin that threatens to fill his face. "I knew there was a reason why I keep you close." He takes a drink before passing it around the rest of the group. Each takes a drink from the bottle until it finally reaches me. I am curious, having never drank whiskey before.

Yaelor finishes her gulp and smiles as she passes it to me. "It tastes weak," she states. "The spirits we drink would strip the hair from your chests."

I take the bottle from her. Only a small dram remains, and I bring it to my lips and let its contents slide down my throat like syrup. My mouth explodes with the smoky oak flavour, which rasps my throat, and I am unable to suppress the cough that escapes my lips. I am amazed at how the others have kept a relatively straight face when drinking it, as I am fighting the urge to let the taste contort my face.

Vireo laughs. "In Levanthria, we say it will put hairs on your chest. It's fine whiskey like that that makes a man."

Gillam casts him a scowl that threatens to drive her dagger into him, the women of the group clearly holding their own when it comes to whisky drinking.

"And women," he corrects himself nervously.

Our final toast done, a warmth remains in my chest that I find comforting, and I stare out through the gaps in the boarded-up window. There is minimal light outside which will work in our favour, with only the occasional lamp burning, a gentle glow emitting around them. Night bugs dance around them in the sky, attracted by the light and warmth that they bring.

"The path looks clear." Gillam searches through the gaps in the windows on the other side of the door. "This will be our best chance to gain entry without being spotted. Remember to stick to the shadows as best as you can."

"Are we ready?" I ask, reaching for the handle of the door.

Vireo gives me a nod and I pull the door open towards us, the breeze from outside refreshing as it rushes inside the tavern. Vireo leads the way while I take up the rear, keeping lookout. If I thought the smell of damp was bad inside the tunnels and the tavern, it pales in comparison to the stench of the muck-lined streets that greet us.

Askela sits in ruin, the streets and houses of this once thriving city more decrepit and broken than the last time I was here. It would appear that the slum's boundaries have expanded farther than I thought possible. My stomach retches, so I bring the cloth of my tunic over my face. The streets are empty, barren of life, though the first few houses are lit by candlelight from within, a rare luxury for these people. I am ashamed to see Askela in such a state of disrepair, ashamed that our former king allowed this fate to befall his people.

Above, the moon is hidden by thick shrouded clouds, causing large shadows to form in between where the lamps are lit.

"Over here." Gillam ushers us into a ginnel, and we line the walls whilst she peers around the corner. "There are two guards ahead, they face away from us."

"Perfect." Vireo pulls on Killian's arm, and the two disappear around the corner. There is an eery silence that hangs in the air, one that I find discomforting, but it is quickly replaced by the stifled grunts of the guards as Vireo and Killian dispatch them from behind. I hear the sound of shuffling feet before the two of them return, dragging a guard each into the darkened ginnel.

They quickly remove the chainmail as well as the black and gold colours of Askela, then get dressed into it themselves.

"See you at the gates," Vireo says before the two of them disappear once again.

We allow a short period of time to pass before we make our next move, drawing closer to the gates that will bring us to the castle courtyard. Memories of Codrin lashing my back resurface, an incident that left its mark on me forever.

The castle gates now in eyeshot, we move towards them, Gillam leading the way. We stand with our backs to the wall as Gillam removes one of her daggers and taps it lightly three times against the wrought-iron gates.

With bated breath, we wait for what feels like an eternity before they slowly start to open. They creak and groan louder than I would like, my own anxiety spiking as we wait to gain entry. As soon as there is enough of a gap for us to crouch under, we make our move. My cloak tears as my hood catches on one of the spikes at the bottom of the gate.

"Shit," I whisper.

We wait within the arches of the courtyard for a sign of Vireo and Killian, the anticipation near killing me. At any moment, guards could descend on us in an instant, outnumbering us. My chest pounds like a beating drum, my breathing heavy.

"What are you doing?" a voice hisses as a guard dives out from beyond the wall. I bring my hand to the hilt of my sword, ready for a fight, my heart spiking.

"Prick!" Gillam scolds. "Are you wanting to meet the end of my blades?"

She pushes the guard and I quickly realise that it is in fact Killian, his face dashed with blood. Within a moment, Vireo joins us, panting from whatever brawl they have just engaged in.

"The entrance to the dungeons lies at the base of the tower on the far side of the courtyard," Jordell whispers, his blackened hand pointing us to our destination. "It is a truly wretched place."

"We will stand guard here," Vireo says, "to keep up appearances. Will you be okay with the four of you?"

"We don't have much choice, do we?" Gillam says. "Try not to draw too much attention to yourself, Vireo."

"You know me."

"Exactly."

The two nod towards one another and Gillam leads us across the outer edge of the shadows to the foot of the tower. She pushes the door open and disappears into the darkness. Jordell, Yaelor, and I quickly follow.

25

JORDELL

"These pathetic lords and baroness' think they can stop me from taking control of Levanthria. I was promised to be Queen by King Athos Almerion, I have the proof that I did his bidding. I have come too far, worked too hard to lose the throne at this stage.

I WILL DO whatever it takes, that is the difference between me and the others."

DIARY ENTRY OF LADY MORGANA, 255 KR

THE FACT that I am in this deplorable place once again weighs heavily on me. On this night, I swear to the gods that one day this tower will fall. The torture that Morgana oversaw here whilst I was working for Jareb was unhinged and abhorrent. I dare not lend my thoughts to the levels of depravity that has fallen on those banished to these dungeons in the subsequent years since my escape.

The smell is foul, forcing all four of us to gag and retch as we make our way down the sodden first corridor. Echoes of drops of water ring down the winding passageways as we descend the first flight of slippery stone steps.

"What is that smell?" Laith asks.

It is truly vile, the stench of death and decay blended with the fragrance of emptied bowels and soiled clothes. My eyes burn, my nose stinging from the repugnant smell. "Death," I answer curtly.

Morgana needs to pay for what she has done, the depths to which she will stoop to get whatever she desires is truly terrifying.

Ahead of us there is a guard on patrol, and as we reach the bottom of the staircase he walks past the opening. In a flash, Gillam is by his side and slides her dagger across the front of his neck, spilling his blood. He gargles through her tense fingertips which are wrapped around his face to dampen the sound of his death. She lowers him to the floor, his gargled breath ending as I step across his body. His lifeless eyes are wide with shock, his face frozen.

"This way," I tell the others, and we make our way to the jailor room. As we enter, a large, hulking man looks up at us, startled by our appearance.

"The fuck are you?" he asks, reaching for his axe. Gillam rushes at him, but the jailor swings his axe brutally at her, causing her to duck out of the way. Yaelor drives her hatchets towards him, but the jailor swings the heel of the axe, butting her in the face and sending her clattering into Laith.

The two of them slam against a wall as the jailor locks eyes on me. Raising his axe above his hulking frame, he bares his blackened teeth and rotting gums. Then his eyes widen as Gillam drives her blade into his back, and he stoops forward, his axe starting to fall. Laith and Yaelor both rush forward, Laith lowering the dead jailor and Yaelor grabbing the axe, preventing it from clattering to the ground. There is a silence for a moment as we listen down the corridors. If the guards heard the commotion, we would be able to hear them descending on us.

Gillam rolls the jailor onto his back, his skin coated with a blackish blue grime.

"Just how long has he been down here?" she asks, patting him down.

Given his pale skin and dishevelled appearance, I would hazard a guess that the jailor very rarely left his position. After a moment, Gillam finds the keys attached to his belt.

"Come on, let's go," she says, heading down the next corridor.

There is a mixture of barred cells and full-fitting doors. With a click, Gillam starts to unlock each one while Yaelor and Laith open the doors in her wake, searching for the fae.

"How will we know they are fae?" Laith asks.

"Trust me, you will know." I tell him. As I follow Laith into one of the cells, I can't help but gasp with horror at the sight before us.

A man lies dead, his skin as pale as ice, his eyes sunken deep into his face. His body is a bag of bones, his skin pressing down on him as his body has diminished as though he sinks into the ground. I swat the flies that buzz around the room and empty the contents of my stomach when I see the maggots crawling about the dead man's face.

"Monsters, they are monsters," Laith hisses. "Left to this fate all because they can't pay taxes."

"No one deserves this fate." I kneel next to the body and utter a prayer for him. At least he will be at rest in the afterlife. "Come, we must move quickly."

The next cell contains two more bodies and my heart wrenches. "Why would they keep the bodies down here, why would they not lay them to rest?"

"Because she is evil," Laith spits.

If this is what Morgana has allowed to happen to her own people, then she truly does walk down the path of evil. Yaelor looks just as shocked as Laith, her face paling. No amount of training or upbringing can prepare one for such horrors.

"These cells, the people are alive!" Yaelor stands in front of a barred door. Inside are three women, their bodies frail and broken

"Please help us," one of them begs. She is missing a hand, another an eye. The third woman seems to be in a better condition than the others.

"I am sorry for your turmoil, I truly am," I say as I take the woman's trembling hands in my own.

"Please help us. My sisters, they are too weak to exit without aid."

"I will help them," Yaelor offers. "Come, I will lead you to the gates."

"There's too many," Gillam calls, leading a group of broken souls back to us. They shuffle behind her as if they are not of this earth, following blindly to their deaths for all they know.

"Thank you," a weary voice whispers as they pass.

"We can't let them leave alone, it will likely draw attention," Gillam points out. "I will head to the gates with Yaelor. We will guide them to safety." She darts ahead and starts ushering the prisoners back up the stairs.

"We still need to find the fae," Laith says. "Does anyone know anything of the fae?"

"I don't know about the fae," says one dishevelled man, "but there are things they do on the lower level to us." No sooner has he finished the words, the hollow echo of a scream reaches us from below. It sends a shiver of cold down my spine.

"Laith, we will continue our search. Gillam, Yaelor, we will meet you by the gates," I say. The two of them nod and leave to help the prisoners with their escape.

In the last cell, I find an elderly man who has been left behind, too frail to stand. He moves his hand in desperate reach of me, his bones cracking with the effort.

"Release me," his cracked voice wheezes, "I beg you."

I enter the cell and take hold of his cold hands in both of my own. For how long has this man suffered? For how long has he rotted away in this cell? There are few ways worse to die than starvation, and it is clear that this broken man's body has eaten every morsel of fat and muscle he once carried.

"It's okay, I am here with you," I reassure him as Laith comes to the door of the cell.

"Jordell, is everything okay?"

I turn, tears filling my eyes from the pain these people have endured, but also out of anger. This man is too close to death for me to save him, but I will do what I can to ease his suffering. I channel my magic, a warmth cascading down my arms and travelling from my hands to his. His eyes widen for a moment and there is a brief spark of life there. In that moment, I see the strong, wilful man he once was. He breathes in deeply, free of any strain or rattle.

"Thank you," he says clearly, his burden taken away from him. A short exhale of breath passes, and he is released from this world, from his pain.

A sharp pain courses through my arm as the corruption grows stronger, and I grimace at the agony that greets me. It is as though white-hot fire has replaced my blood, forcing my fingers to temporarily lock as though I attempt to grasp something tightly in my hand.

"Jordell!" Laith rushes to help me to my feet. "You can't use your magic! I fear for what it is doing to you."

"I understand that it breaks my body, but I could not allow that man's suffering to continue." I wipe the tears from my face, a tight knot forming at the base of my throat. "We must continue."

When we reach the stairwell, the screams arise again, then dampen to nothing more than a murmur.

It grows darker as we make our way deeper into the dungeon. I find it hard not to slip on the moss and mould that creeps over the stone here. We are deeper than I have been before; I'd never realised how far down these dungeons actually go.

At the bottom, a long corridor is lined with doors, torches hanging three doors apart, lighting the path. A larger glow emits from a doorway at the end of the hall. More agonised screams chase down the corridor towards us.

"We need to do something." Laith picks up the pace as he storms ahead, neither of us checking on the cells that we pass. We can always check them on our way back.

At the end, Laith bursts through a doorway, and for once, I don't bother to caution him against rashness. Someone needs our help.

A faerie hangs from the wall, his hands chained above his head as though he is a prized trophy. He is smaller than the fae folk I met in the forest, about the size of a child. His bare chest is littered with cuts and bruised skin. The biggest difference is the clear wings that protrude from his back. They hang limply, but they are definitely wings. His head is bowed to his chest, and I fear for a moment that we are too late. Suddenly his chest heaves with laboured breath. Another scream reaches us from the next room, and the faerie raises his head wearily.

I raise a finger to my lips to ask the faerie to keep quiet as we step inside. At the far side of the darkened room, a robed mage stands with his back to us, his attention fixed onto something on the table in front of him. Upon the table, legs fight against bindings as a shrill scream escapes the prisoner's lips. With a crack, the mage yanks on something, then raises it above him to inspect it in the light. It is a bloodied wing, torn from the faerie he is torturing.

Laith removes his dagger and makes his move as the mage sets the torn wing down. He grabs hold of the mage and drives his blade into him forcefully, and I hope he feels every part of the cold steel as it enters him. My darkened thoughts shock me, but for what this mage has done in this tortured hellscape, he deserves this final moment.

He fights back, swinging his elbow at Laith, but Laith stands firm and presses the blade even deeper, the mage's bones crunching from the force. As the mage slumps forward onto the table, he knocks over a vial. My breath freezes as I recognise the black substance inside.

It smashes against the stone floor and a blast of shock energy erupts with furious force. It sends me hurtling to the ground, the room engulfed in magic as if we are in the midst of a wild storm. Gusts of strong wind and compressed air swirl around us, cracks of forked lightning darting around every inch of the room. Then as quickly as it started, it stops, leaving nothing but dust dancing in the air.

"What was that?" Laith exclaims as he drags himself to his feet. He starts untying the bindings on the tortured faerie in front of him.

I rush towards the faerie hanging from the wall and do the same.

"Whatever it was, they will have heard it. We need to get out of here, and fast."

26

LAITH

The bindings on the faerie are tight, and her feet have turned purple from the pressure. Her face is bruised and swollen, her skin a pale, yellowish orange.

"Vereyous praise you," she stutters. I know not of the word she uses, but I lift her delicately in my arms, as she is too injured to walk.

"We are here to help you," I tell her, wishing I could assist with the pain.

The other faerie is slumped into Jordell's arms.

"Are you able to walk?" Jordell asks him.

"Yes," the faerie gasps as Jordell helps steady him. His skin is a darker tone than the woman's. "Thank you. I'm Pite, this is Troya. We must help the others! I need to find my husband!"

Jordell takes the keys and shows them to the faerie. "Then we need to move quickly. We do not have much time. Do you know anything of Aruya?"

The faerie shakes her head before Jordell gives me a nod, then the two of them head out of the room and back down the corridor.

"Don't worry, I've got you," I tell the faerie, carrying her from the room as we retrace our steps. Jordell and Pite start opening the cell doors in quick succession. Fae and faeries leave their prisons, iron restraints clasped tightly around their wrists. They appear famished and malnourished, their bodies just as broken as the humans we have already helped escape.

"I will take her to safety, then come back and help with the others," I tell Jordell. I push ahead and begin my ascent up the stairs, eager to get out of this wretched place as quickly as possible. By the time I reach the ground floor, my legs burn deeply from carrying the faerie at speed, but I am more determined than ever to get these people to safety.

I cling on tightly to the faerie in my arms, her stifled breaths a constant reminder of how close to death she is.

"You are going to be okay," I tell her, but in truth it is myself that I am reassuring. I am not going to let any of these souls pass on this night. These dungeons have taken enough. Morgana has taken enough.

The entrance to the dungeon lies just ahead.

"Going somewhere?"

The broad, gruff voice stops me in my tracks. It is one I recognise in an instant, and I turn to find its owner.

"Lek." I stop in the doorway, staring into the torch-lit room. Lek stands there, surrounded by guards.

Beside him, I spot another familiar face: Codrin.

To my horror, Gillam and Yaelor are kneeling on the ground in front of Lek and Codrin, their faces bloodied, Gillam's hair matted with blood.

"Just where exactly do you think you're going with our faeries?" Codrin asks, his pointed nose raised as though he is repulsed by me.

"They deserve better than this, you are monsters!" I spit. "Let these people go, they bring you no harm."

159

"Well, we can't have people sneaking in here in the dead of night, taking what they want, can we?" Lek sneers. "We need to set an example, make sure no one else feels as brave or stupid as you are." His eyes are bloodshot, the skin around them purple and blotched with small red veins crawling across his face.

"Why, Lek? Why would you do this? You were one of us," I ask, stalling for time. There is nothing I can do in this situation by myself.

"How is that back of yours, all healed up?" He teases me, offering me a smug smile, but his face quickly darkens. "I never asked to be dragged into that forest. Morgana freed me from my naive thought. She has gifted me all of Vireo's land and coin in return for my support."

"I am going to enjoy shredding your skin from your bone once more." Codrin's voice is cold as he stands shoulder to shoulder with Lek.

"I think we can have more fun than that." A grin engulfs Lek's face. "You want to save these people, then you are going to have to make a choice."

Codrin casts Lek a look which tells me he is just as surprised at Lek's words as I am. "Choose?" he says.

Lek moves to Yaelor's side and draws his dagger across the top of her arm. She winces in pain but shows composure and bravery in this moment, not giving the brute the reaction that he desires. I step forward not wanting harm to come to her.

"You like her, don't you? That makes this even more interesting. Vireo's right-hand woman, or one that you have taken a fancy to. Choose who dies, or I will slaughter every single one of them in front of you right now!" Lek roars, hulking over me. I would much rather take him one on one, but that is not an option.

"You're nothing but a pig fucker!" Gillam jeers. "You hold no virtue, no valour, to think I once considered you a brother. And you thought you caught me, I've waited for years to be this close to you." Gillam jumps to her feet, slamming the back of her head into Lek's face. A satisfying crunch assures me that she has just broken his nose.

Lek stumbles backwards, a deep growl rumbling from his chest. Taking Gillam's lead, Yaelor throws her elbow back into Codrin's groin. He lurches forward cupping his manhood. It is Yaelor's turn to throw her head back and she greets Codrin's face, albeit not as fierce as Gillam, but Gillam has years of pent-up anger to motivate her. The room falls into chaos as Gillam attacks Lek in a flurry of blows. He stumbles backwards but he is hulking in size compared to her. With a snarl, he grabs hold of her wrist before slamming a boulder-like fist into the side of her face. Gillam takes the blow, simply offering Lek a smile before flipping backwards, kicking Lek in the chin in the process. His head snaps back before he shakes off the blow and lunges for her.

With the faerie in my arms, I am unable to act quickly enough to come to Gillam and Yaelor's aid, and two other guards block my path.

On the other side of the room, Yaelor ducks a blow from Codrin who looks less than pleased, his eyes wide with frustration as he swings again, this time landing a blow to her side. As Yaelor leans into it, Codrin wastes no time gripping the side of her head and tossing her into the wall with a thud.

Lek reaches for his great axe in his pursuit of Gillam, and Codrin removes his sword from his waist. The two of them move with surprising ease, and with weapons drawn against Yaelor and Gillam, they have no option but to raise their hands in submission. Gillam gives Lek a wry smirk as he growls in frustration at her before grabbing her by her hair and throwing her in front of him once more. Codrin does the same with Yaelor who continues to show she is just as fierce as Gillam.

Enraged, Lek puffs his chest out, demonstrating his hulking frame. "I have no need for valour, I have all of Vireo's land. I have his manor, and all the pleasurable company I could ask for." Lek places his axe to his side and draws on a dagger from his belt. "I said choose!" he growls at me. "Pick one. That's all you have to do, and I will let the rest of you leave."

Codrin frowns at Lek in disapproval, but says nothing.

"Choose?" I ask, shocked by what he asks of me.

"What is going on here?" Jordell finally reaches me and catches a glimpse into the room at the horror that is unfolding.

"Take her," I tell him, passing the injured faerie to him. "Get them out. Now!"

"Laith –"

"Go!" I roar, and he reluctantly heads to the door with the rest of the fae folk. I am surprised to see neither Codrin nor Lek move.

"Morgana will not be pleased you have let them escape," Codrin says, his sword held against Yaelor's shoulder.

"It will make capturing them again a little more fun," Lek barks back before returning his attention to me. "Now, Laith, you have a choice to make. Pick one to die and the rest live. Do nothing, and they will all die, as will you."

"I'm going to kill you!" I tell him as my chest heaves with the burden of what I am asked. I care for both, how am I able to pick one to live? My mind spins with thoughts of my options. There are simply too many of them for me to fight; it would certainly lead to all their deaths. My eyes throb and a strong headache pounds at my skull as though I have taken a blow to the head. The room falls deathly silent, save for the whimpering of the injured people crowded in the corner. Gillam and

Yaelor breathe heavily in anticipation of what is to come. A lump forms in my throat, making it difficult to take in air.

"Last chance, Laith, CHOOSE!"

My eyes dart from Yaelor to Gillam and back again, a thousand scenarios playing out in my mind. Yaelor smiles and bows her head, as if she understands the decision that I will make. In this moment my heart breaks. Gillam looks me in the eyes and a single teardrop falls down her cheek. She raises her bound hands in front of her, placing her knuckles fist to fist, just like when she confided in me by the campfire. I know in an instant what she means by this. She is guiding me, making the choice for me.

"I'm sorry, I truly am." My voice trembles as I struggle to form words, my eyes welling as I look her in the face. "I choose Gillam."

Gillam bows her head as Yaelor lifts hers up in surprise.

Without hesitation, Lek raises his axe above his head and brings it down onto Gillam's shoulder, near splitting her in half. Her blood sprays across the room, her eyes wide with shock as her shoulder and arm fall away from the rest of her body. She drops face-first to the ground, her blood oozing to form a large pool around her.

The world comes to a stop. It is as if everyone moves in slow motion as I come to terms with the choice I have just made. I feel sickened and shocked to my core, unable to process what I have witnessed. I can only pray that I will wake at any moment from this perpetual nightmare.

"A deal is a deal," Lek says coldly.

Codrin kicks Yaelor towards me and nods to the guards, who allow the prisoners to stumble towards me.

I reach down to help Yaelor up, taking my eyes off Lek for a moment.

"Look out!" Yaelor warns, and I look up just in time to see

Lek's axe bearing down on me. I pull Yaelor out of the way just in time and step back to avoid the blow. My body is acting on instinct, a black void left in my mind, bereft with grief and anger.

"GO!" I shout as Yaelor stumbles out of the room, and the remaining prisoners shuffle after her.

I unsheathe my sword, growling at Lek. It is as if there is only us two in the room. My eyes burn deeply into him. I lunge forward, but Codrin blocks my blade, Lek's snarling face grinning ahead of me.

"Strike again and I will see to it that all of those people out there are dragged straight back to these dungeons."

I pant, my jaw clenched tightly as I envision the satisfaction of driving my sword into Lek's stomach.

"Tell Vireo that he is next, that my axe is waiting for him whenever he is ready."

Clarity grips me from the edge of madness as though I stand at the top of a cliff, waiting to crash into the rocks below. That is what this was about. Lek wants Vireo to react, to leave their camp weakened.

"We will avenge her," I vow before running for the door. No one follows. I race for the exit and find where Vireo and Killian stand watch at the gates, the rest of the prisoners already having passed through.

Nothing can prepare me for the look on Vireo's face as I tell him that Gillam has drawn her last breath.

He screams out in pain, and I grab him, pressing all of my strength against him as he seeks to enter the dungeons alone.

"Vireo, we will avenge her!" I protest. "We need to get the others to safety. We need to get them back to the forest."

My heart breaks for the friend I have lost, the guilt of my choice weighing heavy on me like a suffocating pull into darkness. It breaks even more to see Vireo so bereft, so broken. His sister-in-arms is gone.

I dread his reaction when he learns it was because of me.

27

JORDELL

"*Orjan,*

I have word from a mutual friend of ours in Laith. He wishes to meet with you to discuss some matters. It is of great importance as he seeks clarity that I fear he will not move on from unless he hears it directly from yourself. Personally I do not understand why you draw an alliance with Morgana, but Laith sees good in you. If you wish it also, please head to the outer edges of the forest of Opiya, if you wait by the ravine to the east, our guards will escort you to meet the boy.

I pray that you do not let him down and prove me right."

LETTER TO ORJAN FROM GILLAM, 255 KR

WE TRUDGE through the thick mud that coats the ground, the heavy rain lashing against us, matching the group's darkened spirit. It is a heavy loss of our own that we have faced, and no one has spoken a word on the way back to the Verusha.

There are no smiles on our faces when we arrive back at the camp. Healers rush to tend to the weakened fae and humans we have brought back with us from Askela.

People cheer as though our mission has been a success. Little do they know the price it has cost. Vireo drops from his horse and moves to the centre of camp to speak. Not since Allana's death have I seen him bereft with grief in this way.

"These people have been saved from the dungeons within Askela, but the cost that it has come with is too great," Vireo calls loudly as the members of the camp start to circle around him. "Look a little closer and you will find that our party is missing one. Someone more important to me than they will ever know." His voice cracks, rain cascading down his face, a thunderstorm growing overhead. It is as though he controls the weather as his words ring around the camp.

Killian, Yaelor, a broken Laith, and I line up in the crowd, our heads bowed. My thoughts are with Gillam in this moment, her loss immeasurable to us. Laith's head remains bowed, and given his shortness of breath, it is clear that he is shedding a tear for his friend. The two of them were always close, and I know in my heart the burden he will forever carry from not being able to save her.

Members of the crowd whisper to one another as they slowly start to realise what has happened.

"Gillam, my dear sister-in-arms. A woman who has saved my life far more times than she would have cared to realise, has greeted the afterlife." Vireo's voice breaks once more, and he searches the sky above as he forces the heavy words to escape his lips. "She gave her life for the freedom of others."

"I'm sorry, Vireo," Laith offers an apology that he does not need to offer, and Vireo's eyes lower to him.

Vireo rushes forward and grips Laith by the collar, yanking him close. "You dragged me away when you should have let me face our enemy in open combat," he snarls. Laith's head remains bowed, offering no form of struggle against him. "You stopped me taking vengeance against those who took her from me!"

It is not hatred in his eyes that I see, but grief.

"That is enough!" I bark, slamming my corrupted arm down onto Vireo's, ignoring the pain that shoots up my arm. I break the grip and push Vireo back with my weakened arm. "We are all grieving, Vireo. Her death is not Laith's fault. You have no right to take your grief out on Laith. He feels her loss, too."

"It is, though," Laith says, his eyes still fixed on the ground. "It is my fault she is dead."

I have no idea what he means by his words. How can he be to blame for this?

"They made me choose between Gillam and Yaelor. if I didn't, then they were going to kill everyone."

In a flash, Vireo's face turns to rage, and he dives past me, lashing Laith's face with his fist. "You chose her to die!" Vireo spits, "all so you can lay with a Barbaraq you barely know!" His words are twisted and dark, and I see a flash of the man Vireo used to be. I do not like it.

"Vireo, control yourself!" I demand.

"Control myself? Because of him, Gillam is dead. I have lost the one person who I hold dearest in this world." Vireo points angrily at Laith as I position myself in between the two, knowing that I will not allow him to strike Laith again.

"Think about the situation for one moment," I say. "Think about the impossible situation that he was in. Vireo, you need to grieve, we all do. Perhaps once you have a clear head, this will be an easier conversation to have, no matter how difficult it is."

Yaelor's shoulder are drooped, her spirits broken, no doubt

in the midst of guilt at being the one to survive. Something that I have seen soldiers return from war with. She turns to leave, making her way back to her tent. Vireo's eyes trail after her. He is grief ridden and not thinking clearly; I cannot allow him to make decisions and act on impulse in this state. I fear what he would do to Laith.

"I am sorry, Vireo, I wish I could go back," Laith says. "I wish I could save her, she was my friend, too. It is all my fault." His sobs take control of him. I hate seeing him this way. He has never had to deal with a loss of this magnitude. I can't begin to imagine the guilt he is placing on himself even though the situation was far from his control.

Vireo steps forward as if he is ready to strike, but I puff up my chest and outstretch my arms to show him that I will not let him pass. He starts to draw his arm back but hesitates, his jaw clenched tightly, fighting his own wave of tears.

"At least we have rescued the fae," he snaps, his tone darkened with anger. "No matter what the cost to me."

I understand his frustrations. After all, he did not wish to enter Askela in the first place. I can only hope with time that he will see sense and reason, and that Gillam's sacrifice will ease tensions with the fae. Otherwise, all this would have been for nothing.

"To hell with them!" Vireo spits, "to hell with all of this."

"Come, Vireo." Killian steps forward and ushers Vireo away from the campfire. "We will rest before organising a ceremony for our fallen sister." He offers a bow towards me as he leaves, and I nod in appreciation for him redirecting Vireo away from Laith. I have no doubt he will come to regret the way he has responded, he just needs time to process.

I turn to face Laith and plant both of my hands on his shoulders as he continues to sob. "It is not your fault, Laith."

"It is. I made the decision, I sent her to the afterlife."

I cannot bear to see him this broken and I pull him in towards me, wrapping my arms tightly around him.

He sobs into my chest, gripping me back tightly before roaring in pain into me. Rain continues to bounce off us, the storm showing no reprieve.

"Vireo needs time," I tell him. "You need time." I continue to squeeze him as I try to comfort him as best I can, my words likely offering little to him in this moment of darkness.

"It hurts, it hurts so much, Jordell," Laith's muffled words greet me. For now, I say no more. I just allow the grief to take over, knowing that this is the only way that Laith will process what has happened.

By the time the storm passes, Laith has retired to his hut bereft with the guilt of Gillam's death. As much as I wish to grieve her passing too, I am aware that we have a camp full of fae folk that we must return to their kingdom.

The forest is damp and dreary, the spirits of the camp truly broken. There is no work today, no one harvesting crops, no one tending to the campsite, no younglings at play. Everyone remains mainly indoors as they come to terms with the loss. I have spent my time in the healer's tent, doing what I can to help the injured.

"When will the fae be ready to travel?" I ask a young healer as she helps feed the faerie who has had her wings plucked from her back.

"Troya is the one who is in the worst condition. We have done all we can for her, maybe her kind will be able to offer greater help," the healer says, her sandy hair hidden away under the leaf-filled cloak that she wears.

"I will lead them back to their queen," I say.

The rest of the fae are spread around the healer's tent, some in makeshift beds, others standing in conversation with their kind.

I turn to the fae I'd unchained in the dungeons. "Pite, it is good to see you are recovering well."

He looks at the lifeless body of one faerie who has been covered with a sheet to preserve their dignity. "My husband did not make it. His body was too broken."

"I am truly sorry for your loss."

"It is not your doing," he answers. "At least I will be able to give him a burial."

"Are your people ready to travel?"

"I think so," he says, looking around the room. "Troya is the only one unable to walk, her injuries being the worst. I have never known a faerie to survive their wings being stripped from them. She is strong, however, and hopefully our own healers will be able to help her."

"Ready your people. We head back to your kingdom."

I leave the healer's tent and make my way back to my own to collect my effects. Once the fae queen has her people returned, hopefully she will call an end to the conflict and help me with finding this blasted sword. If I learned anything in the dungeons of Askela, it is that stopping this Great War, stopping Morgana, is even more imperative than I'd ever imagined.

28

LAITH

I sit at the end of my bed, staring into the green canopy outside my cabin. I play the night's events over and over in my mind, each time searching for new answers. Each time torturing myself with what played out. Gillam is dead and it is my fault.

In her final moments, Gillam raised her hands in a gesture I know was telling me to choose her. She sacrificed herself so that the others would be freed. A true act of selflessness, but one that I can't help but feel the guilt of facilitating. Her eyes. Every time it plays over in my thoughts, I am drawn to her deep hazel eyes. Widened with shock as Lek cleaved through her skin with his axe. No amount of bravery or preparation could have prepared me for that. As I stood there staring into her eyes, I saw a fear as she greeted the afterlife. It is a look that will haunt me until the day I leave this world.

Night creeps in to greet me, but I can think of nothing worse than sleeping, so instead I lie on my bed, playing everything over and over in my mind until the sun begins to rise. My clothes are still sodden with the rain, their stench offensive with the fragrance of death from the dungeons. I am still caked in the mud from the journey back to the forest, and my lip throbs where Vireo struck me. My head pounds as though it is encased in its own thunderstorm, a dark cloud hovering over my mood.

I decide that I should head to the lagoon and wash my clothes. Maybe a swim in its waters will aid the headache that plagues me.

The camp is unusually quiet. A woman stands by the cauldron making today's soup for everyone, but other than that no one else is around. I look at the trees at the north of the camp and wonder how Jordell is doing. I could not bring myself to see him as he set off to return the fae folk. I wonder where he draws on his energy levels; I feel as though my own body runs on nothing more than the air I breathe. Being tired but not wanting to sleep is truly torturous.

The walk to the lagoon is but a short distance with nothing more than the rustling trees and hooting owls offering me a brief semblance of company. The ground is sodden, making the terrain difficult, and droplets of water balance intricately on the surfaces of the leaves. Branches soak me once again as I push through them, my mind clouded as I trace over Gillam's final moments once more.

By the time I reach the lagoon, I breathe a sigh of relief and find myself entranced by the water that cascades down the waterfall. The distraction brings a welcome reprieve from my tortured thoughts. The water glows its turquoise blue, the fish glowing brightly as if they are stars themselves. Letting out a sigh, I remove my dirtied clothes and place them by the water's edge before jumping in. The water is refreshingly crisp, not as warm as the last time I entered them but exactly what I need. The slight chill sharpens my breath but centres me in this moment. I feel the thickened ice encased around my mind begin to thaw as I submerge myself under the water. I remain there, appreciating the muffled sounds that surround me, the water crashing from the fall above sending out a constant pulsation of soothing water.

I rise to the surface and flick my hair back, rubbing the dirt from my face. The throbbing feeling in my lip dampens as I bathe. I know not if this is from the healing properties of the water or merely that I feel slightly more relaxed.

I then swim back to the shallower part of the water and start the process of submerging my clothes and cleaning them. If the stench of the dungeon does not wash away, then the only thing these clothes will be good for is fuel for the fire in camp.

After I finish washing them, I place them on the bank and decide to have a swim in the lagoon. A soft haze sits on the surface of the water, and I dive under, swimming until I surface at the foot of the waterfall where I let the waters crash into my aching muscles. When I look out over the lagoon, I notice someone standing by my clothes.

Yaelor.

I make my way to her as she takes a seat at the edge of the pool and lets her feet sit in the water.

"I can't rest," she says.

"Neither can I."

The crescent shape of the moon glows brightly behind her.

"How's your arm?" I ask, drawing attention to her bandages.

"It is nothing that a few stitches could not heal. One of many scars that I now carry." Her eyes sit low. "I know that conflict arose between us, but I am still saddened by Gillam's death. She died a warrior's death. One that the Barbaraqs would be proud of."

"I keep searching the trees, expecting her to walk through at any moment, but that is a fool's wish. She is gone. It is something I will carry with me for the rest of my life." A pang of pain crawls over me, not one brought by a physical ailment but one that sits heavy on my chest, making it hard to breath. It is suffocating.

"Jordell was right in what he said. You were given an impossible choice. My struggle is understanding why you chose me and not her." Yaelor is pained by her words, her hardened exterior fractured.

"Gillam helped me. She told me, in her way, to choose her. She wanted me to choose her."

"She did not speak any words in her final moments."

"It was a gesture, a symbol she made with her hands. One that she told me grounds her. I knew in that moment what she asked of me."

"Thank you," she says, and a tear runs down her face, dripping into the lagoon.

"I do not deserve your thanks," I say, and this is a true belief that I hold.

"That is twice now that you have saved me from the brink of death." Yaelor removes her feet from the waters and stands above me. The crisp air sits upon her skin as though she glows as brightly as the moon above. She reaches for the back of her top and undoes the clasp, letting it fall to the ground before lowering her pants. Something feels different. She looks deeply into my eyes as she removes her clothing, and my chest starts to pound against my ribs. I am transfixed, my own eyes not shifting from her gaze, not even tempted to look at her naked form. She steps forward, lowering herself into the water. The coldness seems to catch her breath as she moves towards where I stand in the water.

I don't know what to think or do. I think I know what is about to happen but given how I have reacted previously, I cannot be sure.

Stop overthinking! I scold myself and I allow myself to be consumed in the moment. A deep longing courses through me, a pressure from the top of my head all the way down to my groin. It is as though sparks of lightning fork through my veins as my senses are heightened. The rippled water reaches me, tickling my chest.

Yaelor stops in front of me, our breath searching for one another. We are surrounded by a thickening mist as though the temperature in the water is raised by our presence. Yaelor raises her hand and delicately brushes her fingers across the top of my scarred shoulder, my body shuddering at the gentle touch as she lowers her hand down to my abdomen. It is as though she wields sparks, my skin tingling far beyond where she touches, and I groan slightly. Yaelor raises her head and looks me deep within my eyes again, and I cannot restrain myself any further. I lower my face to hers and greet her lips with my own, her mouth warm and comforting.

She raises herself in the water and wraps her legs around me. I grab hold of her with both my hands and hold her in place as we passionately kiss one another. She pulls away from me and charms me with a smile. This is a moment I wish we could stay in for eternity. Then she lowers herself down onto me and we groan together in delight. We start rocking back and forth in the water, gentle and slow, gathering pace.

Yaelor presses her body as close to mine as she can, and I feel her heart beat wildly against my chest. Water ripples around us as we steal each other's breath, my head feeling as though it will explode at any moment, awash with sensations I have never experienced before. Our bodies intertwined, I use my arms to raise and lower her, each time a louder groan escaping her lips. This only serves to invigorate me as we speed up, the rocking motion causing waves around us. Yaelor presses her head into my neck and I feel her teeth bite down onto my shoulder as I squeeze her hips tightly. She tightens her hips and draws me in even closer to her, something I didn't think was possible, and with a groan we both release at the same time. My chest thunders as we race to catch our breath. Yaelor lightly presses her forehead against mine, and I hold her steady in this moment.

Just for a little while, I forget the nightmare that the day has brought.

29

JORDELL

"We have proposed a meeting between the Lords and Baroness' to see if we can reach an agreement by way of nominating who should ascend the throne. I have a feeling that this process could take sometime to organise. Reluctantly I think we need to also invite the Great Temple."

Letter to the court of Byron, Coratios Vex, 255 KR

My body grows tired, frail and weak from the journey, but I push through in order to lead these people to safety. The ache in my arm has become unbearable, my skin hot to the touch as though I am gripped by a fever. The air is thick and muggy. I thought it would clear once the storm passed, but it has only gotten worse as we have gotten closer to the fae kingdom. To my joy, I finally recognise the outskirts of their civilisation as the walkways arrive into sight. We have barely stopped since we left Vireo's camp, but I am in dire need of a rest as I come to the conclusion that I am getting too old for this.

My spirits are lifted when the sound of a horn bellows from above, birds fleeing from their trees to flutter in strange patterns before flying off in a different direction in disapproval. The horn blows again, and for the first time I see the fae folk that I escort smile. It is a welcome distraction from my pain, and in that fleeting moment the empathy I feel for what they have been through makes me feel as though it is all worthwhile.

Then my mind traces to Gillam and guilt overcomes me. These people are here ready to be reunited because of her.

The fae folk speed up their walk, some even moving at a steady jog, speaking to each other in fae tongue as they point and laugh, preparing to be reunited with their loved ones. Seeing their smiles and joy is warming and with that my own internal conflict ignites once again. What I wouldn't give to have a simple day where nothing significant was to happen, where I could sit idly and read through my spellbook or any other book for that matter, simply for the joy of it.

A chorus of cheers rings around us as the fae people greet our arrival, ecstatic at our return as we walk through the large wooden gates that lead into the courtyard. A couple of fae higher up wave frantically from the trees, and it takes me a moment to realise it is me they wave at, it is me they offer their smiles to – a far cry from my first experience with them when I was greeted with nothing but wild snarls and strikes to the head.

Queen Zariah greets us at the entrance way to the fae kingdom. "Ready our healers," she commands without delay. Her face is a conflicted picture of sorrow, worry, and joy. She embraces her people as they kneel before her. I follow suit, feeling it best to remain in keeping with their etiquette which appears not too dissimilar to our own.

"Where is Aruya?" the queen asks, "where is my daughter?"

It is Pite who steps forward to speak. "When they captured us, she fought valiantly to protect us."

Beside him, a kneeling fae warrior carries Troya in his arms.

"I have not seen her since we were taken. When they captured us, they tortured us. The things they do in that dungeon are far darker than I thought humans capable of." Pite's voice cracks as he relives his trauma. "They have stripped Troya of her wings. They took Krey and placed him in some kind of flame-filled chamber, rendering him into nothing but ash. Then they used his ashes to create dust, and with it they cast Krey's magic."

Queen Zariah inspects the elixir I brought her. "Tell me, is this what it looked like?" she asks.

Pite nods, shaken. "Where did you get that? That is what they used to put Krey's ashes in."

The queen lowers her head and she sobs to herself, a harrowing wail leaving her that fills the clearing around us. Around me, the fae avert their eyes from their bereaved queen's pain.

"I am sorry, my queen, I truly am," Pite offers.

The queen composes herself before addressing her people once more. "The healers will take care of you. Thank you for the bravery you have shown." Her voice falls deep and flat, her expression wounded but stoic. The returning fae head up the walkways to seek treatment.

I remain bowed in my position.

"You do not need to bow." She places her finger delicately on my chin and raises it. I stand to greet her and bow my head as a courtesy. "Queen Zariah, we were able to rescue your people, as you can see. Unfortunately, not all made it. Our camp also lost one of our own during the rescue."

"I see a sadness in your eyes," Queen Zariah observes, her empathy clear by her pained expression. "Were you close to the person who did not survive?"

I nod. "She was one of the people who created the camp on the other side of the forest. She will be a heavy loss to our group. Her legacy will live on. Her name was Gillam. She was as fierce and brave a warrior as I had ever had the pleasure of calling my friend."

"Gillam. She shall be known as the person who helped bridge the gap between human and fae, alongside your own. My people will sing her name in celebration tonight, and her song will be sung throughout our history." The fae queen grows teary once more, her eyes welling as though they are a dam ready to burst at any moment.

"I am so frightfully sorry for your loss." As I speak, my legs suddenly give way, my body too weak to stand. I plant my foot and brace myself in a kneeling position, preventing myself from collapsing into the dirt. I call out in pain, resting my corrupted arm on my knee.

"The corruption in your arm takes its toll. Let me see." Queen Zariah rushes towards me and steadies me as she draws my sleeve above the elbow. The thick black veins bulge as though they are ready to burst at any moment, my skin cracked and weeping dark blood like it is a charred piece of wood in a fire, barely any unblemished skin visible. As the queen raises my arm to inspect it further, I grimace as an all-too-familiar shooting pain rides up my arm to my chest, shortening my breath. I grit my teeth together, the temptation to bite down on my hand becoming all too much, to help distract me from the pain. Zariah grabs the collar of my tunic and rips it, revealing my bare chest.

"It has spread beyond your arm," she states as she stares at the worsening corruption. "Do you realise how close to death you are? If that corruption reaches your heart, you will be of this world no longer."

I close my eyes, desperate for the pain to end. "Take it," I say. I see no further option. "Take my arm."

The queen mutters to herself as if she disapproves of me letting my arm get like this.

Panic overcomes me as a searing pain engulfs my chest. The corruption seems to be spreading at an accelerated pace towards my heart.

"P-please," I stutter. "Take it. Make it stop!"

"It will make no difference," she says, her voice full of empathy. "I am afraid the corruption is too far gone. Your magic has broken your body. You should be thankful it is not your mind."

Soon, it seems, I won't have a mind, either. The realisation of my own peril dawns on me. The corruption draws towards my heart and when it reaches it, my life will end.

"Oh," I say, deflated and accepting of my fate. "If this is how the gods will it. At least Laith has grown into a fine young man. He'll be okay. I can rest knowing I have done my job with him, and he will continue the work that I have started."

"You have faith in your gods, even when you are this close to death." Zariah studies me. "I said removing your arm would not stop the corruption. I did not say I couldn't stop it."

Zariah wraps my cracked, blackened hand with her own. The coldness of her soft, delicate hands feels soothing against my skin.

"What are you doing?" I ask.

Zariah simply looks at me sternly before focusing on my

hand once more. Her hands start to glow a gentle blue as a warmth pulsates from her hands into my own. The glow travels up her arms until her entire body starts pulsating with the same gentle glow of her magic, her skin looking as though it is shining. It is as if she is a goddess, her power transcendent just like her beauty. I sense her pulsating magic tracking about my body. It does not bring me comfort; it is agonising, and I let out a roar of pain, struggling to keep still.

She holds my arm steady with surprising strength, pulling her other hand away. Her fingers contort as her focus remains on the cracked skin across the back of my hand, the point where the corruption started. It is as though her magic latches on to the corruption that engulfs me, like a rope around a wild horse's neck. There is a precise moment where the strange feeling snags in my hand and my wrist cracks loudly from the connection.

Zariah manipulates her fingers in the air as if pulling on an invisible string as she draws on her magic. I notice the strain on her face from the power from which she draws. With a flick of her wrist, the corruption starts to draw from my hand, exiting from the open wound on the back of it. It takes all my self-will to stop myself from passing out from the pain.

Zariah continues to draw on the corruption as it pools into a liquid ball contained by her magic. It swirls in the air as if trying to escape the magic that encases it, aggressively pushing away from Zariah but being dragged back into place by an unknown force.

As I look at my arm, my bulging veins collapse into place and the blackened skin draws back down to my hand as it is dragged from my body. It feels as though fire is under my skin, like the corruption clings to my insides, gnawing at every part of me in desperation to remain.

The blackened ball of corruption is tinged with my blood,

my chest feeling as though it is ready to implode on itself. My head feels faint, a wave of heat washing over me.

"We are nearly there," Zariah says, her focus remaining on my hand. The force of her magic pushes against me as if it is itself repelling me. With one last pull, she tears the corruption from the back of my hand and she lets go of me. I drop to the ground and pore over my arm, which is pale and swollen from my injury – but there is no sign of the corruption.

I pant on all fours as I recover, while Zariah forces the corruption to remain elevated in the air as it desperately tries to escape.

"*Spretu!*" she utters, and the corruption ignites before she slams it to the ground where it burns wildly as though it is made from tar. A high-pitched squeal resonates, threatening to piece my ear drum before it burns motionless on the ground.

The fae queen gathers herself for a moment, mopping the sweat from her head with her sleeve.

"Consider this a gift, in exchange for your aid in returning my people. You will need to rest, but when you are recovered, there is one more thing I wish to share with you before you leave my kingdom."

30

LAITH

We stand by a small pile of rocks that have been piled up in honour of our fallen friend. It has been days since her passing and although we do not have a body to lay to rest, we wanted to create a monument for Gillam in her honour. I stand solemnly, my head bowed out of respect as I draw upon the conversations that we shared within this very camp. Her loss is something that I wonder if I will ever recover from, my thirst for revenge becoming harder to ignore with each passing day.

Yaelor stands by my side. She has been distant since our encounter at the lagoon, but I have not chased her about this or sought another meeting with her, not wishing to offend her or presume that she is mine to take whenever I so choose.

She stands with her hands behind her back, her hair piled high on her head, quiet on her thoughts. She does not show any emotion, unlike the rest of the camp residents that come to pay their respects, their moods sullen and their faces blotched with tears. We stand together to remember Gillam, a torch protruding from the head of her grave. Its flames dance with the wind.

Vireo walks past, his hood raised, his face hidden as he moves to the stones before turning to face us. Once there, he bows his head and lowers his hood, standing quietly as he collects his own thoughts.

He clears his throat before starting to speak. "We are here today to gather in mourning for our dear friend, my sister, Gillam." He pauses, his voice cracking as he speaks. He adjusts himself before starting again. "We are here to pay our respects for Gillam and to celebrate the life that she lived, the life that she gave, so that others could live theirs. An act more noble than most will achieve in their lifetime. Gillam was a person of force, a person so direct with her words that they could carve through stone."

Vireo tilts his head to look at the small stone tower that we have created in her honour and casts it a smile. "She was also fierce, commanding, and loyal. Her counsel has helped us shape this very community. True, we have done things in our past that we would not be proud of, but we have also seen battle together in the name of our fallen king. She has saved me not just on the battlefield but from the demons that plagued my mind long before we laid the foundations for our camp here. For that, I will be eternally grateful."

Vireo fights against his emotions, sniffing back and wiping his face clear of the tears that line his cheeks. "Funnily enough, and believe it or not, we were betrothed to one another by our parents when we were young. Something which we both stringently opposed. It was only when her parents passed that we were able to contest this. As she put it, she would rather bathe in horse shit than marry me."

He laughs to himself and is joined in laughter by Killian and a few others within the crowd. "She threatened to kill me when I first dragged us here, newly exiled. I was sure to keep one eye open at night, for Gillam was one that when she made a promise, she rarely broke it. This one, however I was glad she did, as it enabled me to become stronger and watch with pride as I saw the forest we now call home soften her."

Vireo's voice grows thick and grizzled as he continues his speech, something I give him credit for as I myself would struggle to form the words. "She would stick a knife in from the shadows if she could hear me talking like this." Vireo looks up at the sky and takes a long, deep breath. "Gillam, you are at peace. Know that I long for the day that we can be reunited. I will not rest until Lek pays for his actions. This is my vow to you, my sister."

With this, Virco removes a single white rose from his cloak and kneels by the stone tower, placing it at its base.

"I love you." He closes his eyes and bows his head once more, and we observe a moment's silence until he finally stands. When he steps back, the rest of the camp takes it in turns to place their own roses by her grave: yellow, blue, red, white, orange. It is as though a rainbow has been laid in her honour.

I stare down at the red rose clasped in my hand, and it reminds me of the red cloak she always wore. I rub my thumb up and down the stem, barely noticing that a thorn pierces my skin, causing a pinprick of blood. I step forward, a large knot in my throat, a heavy weight in my stomach as my eyes sting. I kneel and place the rose on top of the others.

"I am sorry, Gillam. In my life, I will help avenge you." I make the blood vow before stepping away from the grave. I am awash with emotions, anger, hurt, grief, sorrow, agony. It is too much for me to process. My chest heaves, and I feel as though I could vomit at any moment.

A hand grabs hold of me, preventing me from escaping as

others leave the graveside. It is Vireo, his face shallow and gaunt as if he has barely slept. I brace myself for conflict, but after a brief moment, this does not happen.

"I needed to speak to you to apologise for how I acted when we returned form Askela," he starts, the look of shame drowning him like a river that has burst its banks. "The way I blamed you, the way I lashed out . . . it is something that does not sit well with me. You have done no wrong in this situation and I was wrong to take out my anger on you."

"You don't need to apologise," I say "I would give anything to be in that situation differently, to act in a way that would have meant she returned with us."

"Do not torture yourself with those thoughts, it will only lead you down a darkened path. You have a big part to play in all of this, of that I am sure. It is not the ending that defines us –"

"It is the path we walk to get there," I repeat, a familiar theme resonating with me that Gillam once shared. The memory of our conversation at this very point draws a smile from me.

"Now will you accept my apology so we can drink wine in celebration of Gillam's life?"

The thought of getting drunk and celebrating feels wrong but also right at the same time. I could quite easily sink a barrel of wine just to aid me in sleep. Maybe that will help me stop seeing her eyes every time I close my own.

Killian marches over with two wooden cups in his hands that are stained red on the inside.

This wine was brewed using Gillam's favourite grapes. I feel it fitting that we toast her life with it. Vireo passes one of the cups to me, then raises his in the air and smiles.

"To Gillam."

"To Gillam," I say, and we clink our cups together before

downing the contents in one go. It is as strong a wine as I have ever tasted, punchy too, a perfect combination to remember my dear friend by.

As we make our way back towards camp, I think about the conversation we had by the fire just a few nights prior, and I can only hope that she has found peace at last.

"Where's Vireo?" a voice calls.

One of the villagers approaches, a spear in his hands. "There is a man at the outer edge of the forest – if you can call him that," he adds. "He has asked after you, Laith."

My heart skips at the mention of my name.

"Who is it?" Vireo asks.

I am sure of the answer before it leaves the man's lips.

"He says his name is Orjan."

31

JORDELL

"The Guild Of Magi offer to help those who possess the ability to wield magic to control their power, to embrace it. Only time will tell what their true ambition is."

VALERAN BUETA, *Scribe to The Great Temple, 253 KR*

I RECEIVE the summons to see the queen after a much-needed rest, my search for sleep granted now that I am free of the corruption. And what a sleep it was, a comforting bed, a thick warm blanket, in a treetop hut suspended by thick vines, and most importantly, no pain. I did not dream, I did not find myself lost in my thoughts, I simply slept and for that I feel more rested than I have felt in as long as I can remember.

Two fae guards escort me, one of which I recognise as the furious fae who captured me when I first found them. So much has happened since that day, my mind and knowledge constantly expanding at what the world has to offer. If the vision of the vast, intricate walkways of the fae kingdom were impressive, it pales in comparison to the castle itself. It appears narrower than the castle in Askela, but once inside, the building is larger than it appears. Whether through magic or a simple trick of the eye, it is a thing to behold. Two large towers stand far higher than anything I have seen before, intricately carved from stone into the shapes of two fae. One is of a woman holding a book, a crown upon her head, her face trans-fixed on the tome that she reads. The other is a male, gripping a sword by the hilt, the blade embedded in the ground in front of him. His face is stern and warning. It is as though the statues are two sides of a coin, opposites of one another. A warrior and a scholar.

The towers seem to be carved from mountains, their great height truly a spectacle. I could have observed them in detail all day, but I can only take in the detail briefly as I am escorted to see Queen Zariah.

Inside the throne room, I stand in awe of my surroundings. The walls are of the same white stone as the exterior, and spiralling columns stand at symmetrical points throughout the room. The furnishings are carved from deep-brown mahogany that contrasts prominently against the bone-white walls.

A large black and silver tapestry flows on the ground from the entrance of the room all the way to the steps that lead up to where Queen Zariah awaits me on her mahogany throne. The images stitched into the thick rug tell a story: stars, ships, fae, and humans have been intricately etched into its surface. Perhaps if the queen allows it, I will have time to study it in depth later.

"How are you feeling?" Queen Zariah asks, bringing me back into the present. Fae guards stand just a few feet behind her, their spears drawn to their sides, ready to protect their queen at any moment.

I bow my head to her in greeting. "Apologies, Queen Zariah," I start, "it is just, this castle, this room, it is truly a mark of perfection." I am in awe of the craftsmanship, having never seen anything to this level created by man. "I feel much better, as fresh as when I first greeted adulthood, though I care not to divulge how long ago that was." I smile at her, grateful for her intervention.

"I am glad you have recovered. You showed my people a great kindness despite the risk to yourself. It was the least I could do to express my gratitude." The queen stands from her throne and moves down the steps towards me. Her footsteps echo quietly in the chamber, her white dress trailing far behind her. She is a picture of grace, elegance, and serenity. "Would you care to walk with me, Jordell?"

"Of course," I answer without hesitation, eager to see more of the castle.

"There is something that I wish to show you. This way." She leads me to a doorway to the side of the throne room that funnels into a magnificent hallway. The ceiling reaches thirty feet above us, and large windows carved from the stone allow a gentle breeze to greet us as light pours inside. Beyond the windows, I can see the kingdom below reaching down to a canopy of trees that stretch far beyond where my eyes can see. A strong gust of air startles me and I jump to the side of the hall. It does not come from the weather but from the giant birds that whoosh past, their riders fixed to their backs.

Queen Zariah laughs at my reaction, clearly used to the giant creatures hurtling past at such speed. I compose myself and continue to follow her.

"The problem with your magic, as you well know, is that your human body was not made to wield it. Every time you do, it breaks down the very fibres that create you. For the fae, we draw our magic from the forest, meaning when we call upon its power it does not wear us down as it does you. It does not threaten to fracture our minds. I want to show you how it all connects, how it is all possible."

She leads me further down the corridor until we reach an opening and step out into what I assume is the palace gardens. My jaw almost slams against the ground at what I see as we exit the palace. A pale oak tree as wide as the castle towers reaches high up into the sky, so much so that I wonder if it surpasses the sky into the very heavens. Its bark shimmers in the light as if decorated with silver.

"The Elder Tree," I breathe, my eyes wide with wonder. It seems impossible for a tree to be this large.

"The source of the magic that enshrines this forest," Queen Zariah confirms. She steps towards the tree and places her hand against the surface, smiling warmly as if sharing her thoughts with it. "Touch it."

I reach out my hand tentatively and place my palm against the bark. It is as hard as stone, the roughness of the bark like calluses. It is warm to the touch, and a comforting feeling falls over me similar to when Queen Zariah gripped my hand to rid it from the corruption.

"Concentrate your mind, try to feel beyond the surface."

Closing my eyes, I focus my senses. The rustling trees, the wind around us, my own breath, my own heartbeat. Then the sensation of another beat greets me, pulsating through my hand. I open my eyes in shock, pulling my hand away in surprise. The sensation stops.

"The tree – the tree has a heartbeat," I stammer. I place my hand against the surface once more, as if madness has overcome me. Once again, the warming beat throbs against my open palm.

"Not a heartbeat, but magic. It courses through this tree, through its roots into the ground. This is where we draw our magic from, this is where the forest draws its magic from." She stretches her arms out and places her pointed ear against the surface, as if embracing a family member. ""I am four hundred years old, still considered a young queen. But this tree is older than anything else in these lands. It is descended from the gods," she says.

"How?" My mind is filled with so many questions.

She smiles, brushing her long dark hair behind her ear. "Opiya, the great goddess of life, had two children. A son, Rhagor, and a daughter, Zariah, who I am named after. It is said that Opiya created these lands as an escape, a place of tranquillity and safety for her and her children. As Rhagor and Zariah grew older, Opiya soon came to realise that although her children had been raised the same, they had two very different personalities. Zariah, full of love and a longing to learn, and Rhagor, full of a thirst for power unquenchable by staying within the forest."

Zariah begins to pace with her hands clasped behind her back. "Rhagor frequently ventured out of these lands, much to Opiya's displeasure. It is said that Rhagor hated his mother for bringing him here. Over time, Rhagor influenced man, and through his manipulation, great wars raged, not just throughout Levanthria but to the wider reaches of the world. The only person who could reach Rhagor, the only one he considered his equal, was his sister.

"Opiya begged Zariah to help stop Rhagor before he destroyed the word as they knew it. Zariah reached out to Rhagor, and asked for him to return home after not seeing him for hundreds of years. Seeing no other way to stop her son, Opiya encased him in stone, but not without its consequence. For Rhagor had sensed that it might be a trap he was walking into, and as such, he bound his power to a blade he had carried since his father's passing. Zariah did not know of Opiya's trap, and although she protested against their mother, Rhagor was incensed, his heart broken at the perceived betrayal by his loving sister."

"As his body stiffened and his skin turned to stone, Zariah embraced him one final time. In his final act, Rhagor did the unthinkable and used his sword to strike down his sister. Broken and dismayed by what Rhagor had become, Opiya dragged the sword from her son's hardening hands and drove it deep into his chest as her magic took control of him. It was too late for Zariah. The sword, enriched with Rhagor's power, was strong enough to kill a god, and as her life slipped away, Opiya did the only thing she could think of to preserve her. Zariah became one with the land, and as her body perished, this very tree grew from her remains, rich with her magic. Her life continues through her magic within this very tree. And from that tree, a forest grew, and from that forest, everything that you see today."

I stare up at the tree in silence, grappling with the weight of her words.

"There is something I must tell you," I say. "Something that I now believe is linked to the story you have just told me."

"Go on."

"I shared a vision with a powerful sorceress, one that fore-told a Great War between man."

"I have seen men start wars with one another throughout my life. It does not concern the fae."

"That is not all. I saw magic unlike anything ever witnessed in our world before. Magic wielded by a sword, a sword that was embedded in stone."

Zariah places her hand against the tree and closes her eyes as if she listens to it. "If what you are alluding to is Rhagor's sword, then I cannot help you. Opiya hid him, ashamed of what he had become. We know not where he rests, nor his blade."

"I think this blade will prove key in ending the Great War that is to come."

"Heed this warning, Jordell. Do not go searching for something that the gods will to remain hidden."

I do not want to press the matter further and risk angering the queen. I bow my head. "If this is what you will."

"Now, I did bring you here to impart you with a final gift, something of which I am certain the Elder Tree approves." Zariah plucks a large branch from the ground at the foot of the tree.

"This is a gift from the fae, a branch from the Elder Tree, from the goddess Zariah herself. She thanks you for all you have done."

I take the branch, confused by what it offers other than as a staff to aid my walking.

"Have you not listened to the tale I have told you, of the power that this tree possesses?" Zariah scolds me as if reading my mind. Then she offers me a smile. "See for yourself, use some of your magic."

Although hesitant given the corruption that I have only recently overcome, I grip the staff tightly in my hand and stretch out my hand to summon a barrier spell. The connection to my magic feels smooth like flowing water as I cast my magic in front of the queen. There is no euphoric feeling, just as there is no crippling pain when I stop. I do it again, this time summoning stronger levels of power, my magic flowing freely as if I am unbowed, a white piercing light forming at the top of my staff. When I cease my magic, the glow fades, and again I am not greeted by the usual affliction that comes with magic-use.

"The branch that you wield will act as a conduit between you and your magic, connecting your powers to those granted by the Elder Tree. This is the true gift that I bestow on you. Be warned, though: this staff is not indestructible. If you push your magic too far, it will run the risk of breaking, and as such, the affliction you wish to avoid will flood into you once again."

"Thank you, my queen," I say, overwhelmed by such a gift.

"Now you must return to your people," she tells me. "You may tell them that the conflict between our two parties has been resolved."

I am truly humbled by the gift, too speechless to respond. No longer am I burdened with the consequences of wielding my magic.

Not only this, but I also leave with the knowledge that the sword that I have seen in my vision exists.

And I grow ever closer to finding it, and to stopping the impending war before it is too late.

32

LAITH

I feel strange as I stand in anticipation of my former sire and mentor returning. The anticipation brings me a wave of mixed emotion from anxiety right through to excitement. I find myself unable to keep still as I stand beside Vireo at the edge of camp, waiting for Orjan to arrive.

"Are you okay?" Vireo asks.

"I think so, I just don't know how to feel."

"Be warned," Vireo says, "his response towards me will be understandably less favourable."

My hands fidget by my side and I find myself toying with the fabric of my tunic. I opt to take a hold of each hand in front of me to hold them steady before my nerves get the better of me. Killian and Yaelor stand behind us, the rest of the camp instructed to remain in the tents and huts. As much as we want to believe the best in Orjan, we cannot risk the safety of the others. Those on watch are prepared to intervene if they need to.

"This is the first time we have allowed an outsider into our camp without the knowledge that they wish to join us," Vireo

198

says. "I only hope that the message Gillam sent on your behalf resonated with your friend."

So much has happened since the last time I saw Orjan, on both of our parts.

"Blasts," I curse, "What is it that takes so long, I grow tired of waiting."

"Careful, boy." Vireo places a firm hand on my shoulder to steady me. "You are beginning to sound like a younger version of me."

I regain my composure, putting my energy into not letting my thoughts race. There is so much for us to catch up on, so much that I long to learn of his life since we parted ways three years past.

There is movement within the trees and the watchman returns along with two other members of the camp, one at the front, one at the back. Between them stands a man taller than I remember, his armour the yellow colours of Rashouya, just as I recall.

"Orjan." I aim to speak his name quietly but find I almost shout his name. He lifts his head towards me and draws closer. His face is hidden behind a cloth, leaving only his eyes visible. They are not ones that I recall; the yellow centres of them are now diamond shaped like those of a reptile, the whites of his eyes darkened. His skin is hardened, looking as though he is coated with scales.

"It's not him," I say to Vireo. But if it's not Orjan, just who is this impostor?

As the strange man gets closer, his eyes lock on to Vireo and his body stiffens. "Vireo!" he hisses, lunging towards him.

"It's definitely him," Vireo quips as the escorting watchmen grip hold of his arms to restrain him.

Orjan is too strong. He drags them with him as he advances

on Vireo, their feet sliding through the mud that they desperately aim to anchor to.

"Scum!" he hisses again, his voice a combination of anger and pain. "All of this is because of you, I am like this because of you!" he roars. He has no weapon, which I assume he was forced to leave before entering the forest. There is hatred in his eyes, oblivious to his surroundings, oblivious to me.

I step in front of Orjan, slamming my hands against his chest and pushing him back with everything I have. His strength is superior, and he pushes against me. "Orjan, stop!" I demand. "It's me, Laith! Your squire."

There is a moment's hesitation before the possessed look in his eyes softens and he lowers his gaze to me. His eyes dart around my face. I have grown so much since we last saw one another, I wonder if he will recognise me.

"Laith?" he repeats, scanning me head to toe. "It can't be." His rasping voice is far from what I recall, but I can tell from his blemished armour and the way he carries himself that it is Orjan. I can hear the hint of his Rashouyan accent on his words.

"I asked Gillam to send a messenger for you."

Orjan's muscles relax, and he stops pushing against me, dropping his arms by his sides. The watchmen gripping on for dear life release him tentatively.

"You have grown so much," he says. "Why do I find you in the company of rogues and scoundrels?"

"What happened to you?" I ask. "You look so . . . different."

His Rashouyan tunic is the same as he has always worn, though the fabric it tattered and torn, parts of it even stained with blood. His chainmail armour hangs underneath. It is as though he has not dared to wash it in all this time. The smell that follows him is foul, and I think about offering him the use of the lagoon to clean himself.

"Everything went wrong after Vireo and his thugs beat me in the street like I was nothing more than the shit on his shoe. Why is it you side with such scoundrels?" he asks, venom in his words.

"Vireo is different now. He keeps these people safe," I protest, ensuring that I remain in between the two of them. Vireo stands quietly behind me, something which I am grateful for. The last thing we need right now is to antagonise the situation.

Orjan scoffs, turning his head away in disgust. "People like him do not change, they do only what they must in order to get what they want."

"I knew him before, and I know him now. I have witnessed it," I say defiantly. "I understand your hostility, but please know that the words that I speak are true."

"After what he did to me, you side with him?"

"I do not condone what he did to you. I tried to kill him for it."

"He ruined everything for me!"

"And what of me, Orjan?" My temper flares. This is not the happy reunion I had hoped for. "What of the young boy you left behind? I had to learn how to survive. I probably wouldn't have, had I not followed Vireo into this forest."

"I came only to make my peace and to apologise for what I did. For how I behaved. I released you from the burden of being attached to me, from being my squire," Orjan says.

"And in doing so it led me down this path to this moment. I stand in front of you not as a boy but as a man, and as a man, I implore you to listen to me."

"After everything I have been through, everything that I have witnessed, it disappoints me to see you standing by the side of this thug."

How dare he? How dare he look down on me with pity,

how dare he speak to me this way after how he himself has behaved? I find my mood of anxiety and excitement at being reunited quickly turning to one of anger and frustration. "How can you speak of disappointment when I hear stories of your involvement with Morgana? Is it true, Orjan? I have spent years helping search for a sword that can bring about an end to all of this death and destruction that she brings, one that can end a war before it even starts." Words pour from my mouth as years of lost conversation fall from me like a waterfall. "Please tell me the whispers that I hear are not true. Tell me you do not stand side by side with that vile sorceress. Tell me that you do not walk such a darkened path."

Orjan remains silent for a moment, his reptilian breaths deep and untrusting. "Yes, I fought alongside her when Eltera was besieged." Orjan's eyes shift from me to slowly focus on Yaelor. "I see that it is not just scoundrels you harbour in this forest, but savages, too. I could ask if you yourself think you are on the right side of this fight, Laith. From where I stand, it does not look redeeming." Orjan rakes his eyes over Yaelor, anger seeping through the pores of his scaled skin. "I saw the blood that she spilled in the name of her people when they attacked us. It was she who led the charge."

Hushed whispers ring out around us from those that watch on.

"I already know about the attack on Eltera, Yaelor and her tribe were brought there under false pretences."

"Laith, you reprimand me for standing by Morgana's side, yet you harbour her blood in this very camp." Orjan bears his pointed teeth in an act of aggression. "Has she told you that she is Morgana's sister?"

"Lies!" I turn to look at Yaelor who bows her head, shame crawling over her like a creeping shadow. "Yaelor, is what Orjan says true?"

"Laith, if I can just explain – "

"Is what he says true?" I scold her, venom dripping from my spiked tongue that could rival Orjan. Yaelor can barely look me in the eye, and I can tell by the way her shoulders stoop that there is more she is not telling me.

She nods, and a plummeting feeling roots in the bottom of my stomach. "This Morgana who you speak of, she is my sister."

Gasps spread amongst the forest folk like a raging wildfire, their scoffs of disapproval impossible to mask.

"Trust me, Laith, I did not know, nor do I condone the things that she has done."

"No," I whisper under my breath, my legs feeling as though they are plated in steel, ready to buckle at any moment. "How is this so?" Has every moment we shared since our paths crossed been a ploy? To get close to me? To get close to this camp?

"Laith, you have to trust me. I mean your people no harm."

"Trust you!" My voice rises. "How can I trust you when you are of the same bloodline of Morgana, and you kept it from us? From me?"

"Because I knew how you would look at me." Yaelor stands defiantly. "It is how you look at me right now. With hatred in your eyes, in your heart."

"I vouched for you. I saved you. I chose you – " thoughts of Gillam's death threaten to crush me to the ground.

"This is why you called your warriors back from the battle in Eltera," Orjan rasps from behind me. "You discovered you faced your sister on the battlefield."

I spin in a daze, turning my attention back to Orjan, a rage building up inside me.

"How can you condone what Morgana does?" I say my frustration pushing to the forefront of my swirling mind. "We have been into those dungeons, we have seen the torture that she puts her prisoners through. People who she deems crooks and criminals all so she can experiment and improve her power." There is a fire inside me and my blood burns.

"I can only speak of the actions I am able to know as true. I witnessed Morgana fighting for her people, I witnessed her put her life on the line to stop Eltera from falling. Yet I find you here with Vireo, a man wanted by the Crown, and a Barbaraq invader who has recently assaulted the city I now find myself steward of."

"Is that what this is about?" I ask, "all of this, siding with Morgana so you can have a veiled version of honour restored to your name?" I cannot believe what has become of the person I once called a mentor.

"I do what I must to protect the people of Eltera. I will do what I must to uphold justice."

"You must see that Morgana is evil!" I bellow. "She is manipulating you, she must be." I can't see any other reason for why he would side with such a monster.

"I see more clearly now than I ever have, Laith. Perhaps it is you who is blind to your surroundings. I think it is time that I leave."

The guards look on aimlessly, unsure what to do.

Vireo breaks his silence. "You are free to leave, Orjan. Just know that I am sorry for how I behaved, I am sorry for my indiscretions."

"Save your apologies, Vireo. If our paths are to cross again, I will gladly be the one to send you to the afterlife." With this, Orjan turns and heads out of the camp to leave the forest.

I watch in disbelief as he disappears out of sight. Yaelor's warnings were true; Orjan sides with Morgana, and as such, that makes him our enemy. My enemy.

"Should we stop him?" I ask Vireo, unsure of what to do.

"He has not wronged this camp and all I see are words. He is driven by his anger towards me. Hopefully in time he will come to realise the alliance he has forged is a mistake and when he does, we will be here waiting for him."

There is an air of diplomacy from Vireo that surprises me, knowing that he was never a fan of Orjan himself.

"Do you think he will see sense?" I ask.

"We can only hope."

I pray that when this day arrives, it is not too late to save his soul.

I turn to Yaelor while the rest of the camp watches on, whispering to one another, their judging eyes saying everything that their words do not.

"Laith, may I speak to you in private?" Yaelor asks.

"I think you have said enough," I glower, unable to even look at her. Betrayal eats at my core like vultures tearing away at a carcass. I gave myself to her, I let her into my heart and now find it fracturing like a broken mirror. Has everything she said to me been a lie?

"Laith, I am not on her side," Yaelor protests. "I have seen the horrors of her dungeon and I know she needs to be stopped. I am on your side."

When I don't respond, Yaelor spins and walks away towards her hut. The forest folk continue to tut and whisper.

Vireo places a gentle hand on my shoulder, looking me in my eyes. "I can only speak for what I have seen, but I think Yaelor is being honest with you. Don't let your anger ruin what you two have built."

"It's a little late for that," I say, shrugging my shoulder free and heading away from the camp.

It seems that the people I trust the most tend to stab me in the back.

33

JORDELL

"Orjan brings word of Laith, I do not want to tempt fate by crossing paths with him. Not when I have foreseen he is the bringer of my death. I have sent Lek with a message, if Laith surrenders I will offer mercy. If they do not I have instructed Lek to destroy them all. I have even let him take my faerie infused potions to aid him, although I may have remained tight lipped on the the consequences of using them. Using magic naturally has grave consequences on the body so imagine the havoc it rages on someone who uses it un-naturally."

Diary entry of Morgana, 255 KR

With my new staff in my possession, I feel invigorated. It is as though the removal of the corruption has turned back the time on my ageing body. My journey back to camp has passed quickly as I feel as though I am moving quicker through the terrain. When I arrive back, I see Vireo conversing with Killian at a table. Their faces tell me their conversation is serious and I can only imagine what has happened in my absence.

"What is it that brings such a worry to your face?" I ask, interrupting the conversation between the two of them.

"We have had a visitor," Vireo tells me, "one that Laith had sent a message to. And though I understand why he reached out, I fear the danger he has inadvertently placed this camp in."

I know in an instant who it is that he sent for. "Laith sent word to Orjan?" I ask tentatively.

"You knew of this?"

"How would I have known? I have barely been in Verusha of late," I reply sternly. I wish Laith would have spoken to me about this before sending word so I could have talked it through with him.

"I fear that the meeting did not go how Laith had hoped. Orjan sees us as the villains. His hatred for me was apparent, his disappointment in Laith was clear. Heated words were exchanged but Orjan made it abundantly clear that he sides with Morgana."

"Morgana is a master of manipulation. Are you sure that Orjan fully sides with her?"

"Laith told him the things that she has done, of your quest to end this Great War before it has even started. He begged Orjan to see sense, but he did not," Killian adds, taking a drink from his wooden cup.

I take a seat at the table with them, resting my new staff against its side. I rub my fingers against my temple to soothe the headache that is forming. "This is not good. Orjan is a man who prides himself on honour. Rashouyan honour is known for its fierceness. I have no doubt that Orjan will do whatever he must, if he believes it to be honourable."

"Like apprehending a band of wanted criminals?" Vireo

asks. "This is what I fear most, that Verusha, all that we have built over these years, is no longer safe. The problem is, we still do not know what Morgana's end goal is. What it is that she searches for, what she hopes to attain other than the throne?"

"I know her. She has always had a thirst for knowledge and power. I fear that the pieces in the puzzle that lead to the war are beginning to form a picture. There are still gaps, however, meaning that although we are sure she will make a play for the Crown, we do not know what comes next. What she seeks to do with her power."

"What do we do now? There are simply too many for us to up and leave, where would we go?"

"We could send word to the fae," I answer. "Queen Zariah has promised that they will spill no more blood on their lands, that the conflict between us and them is ended. Although I fear asking them to house us may be a step too far. There are lots of fae who do not wish to have humans living within the forest. The queen still needs to keep her people happy and safe and this is but a new relationship that is forming."

"How long will that take though, Jordell? Each time you leave, you are gone for days on end." Killian is right in his concern. "What if they attack the camp whilst you are gone?"

"I feel that the bond between myself and Queen Zariah is strengthened by us rescuing her people. Perhaps she will return that deed back to us if they see that we are under attack. Is this what you think will happen, Vireo? Do you feel an attack is imminent?"

"I saw the look in Orjan's eyes. I fear he will head straight to Morgana and tell her of our location. I fear that it is only a matter of time before they reach our camp."

"Vireo, Vireo!" a voice draws an end to our conversation. A scrawny woman races through the centre of the camp towards us on horseback. Her face is reddened, her thick hair seeming to have captured leaves like a trap. She pants heavily as she steadies her horse in front of us.

"Askelan forces," she speaks hurriedly, out of breath and desperate. "Askelan soldiers march this way. We scouted them to the south, they have numbers larger than ours."

"Are you certain?" Vireo asks.

"Yes. I give us two days at best."

"Thank you," Vireo says, "We need to prepare everyone for what may come."

Morgana wouldn't march on the forest just to apprehend a few wanted criminals. "Morgana must be in search of the sword," I say, the realisation dawning on me. "I have every faith that the fae will lend us their aid. I cannot see them allowing the sword to fall into her hands."

"By the gods, I hope you are right," Killian says, worry etched into every deep wrinkle that adorns his weary face.

The villagers that had been going about their daily lives, tending to wood, the crops, harvest, cleaning, had come to stop when the scout arrived.

With eyes on us, Vireo stands on the table. "Can I have everyone's attention!" he calls out loudly. People around us stop what they are doing in their tracks and begin to convene around us. "We must prepare for an attack on our homes."

There are hushed words between the villagers as they discuss the news.

"As it stands, we have a few options. We flee, to where I do not know, but we leave the forest and search for safety for our people elsewhere in Levanthria."

"But this is our home!" a man calls, his face dirty from his day's work.

"We have built this from nothing," a woman yells, clutching the hands of two children. "This is our home now, we won't let them take it away from us."

To this, a chorus of cheers rises from the group, a strong sense of spirit entwined between them which fills me with pride at what they have built here.

"I had a feeling this was how you would react." Vireo smiles. "This leaves us with two other options. It is myself that is wanted by the Crown, by Morgana. I have been a thorn in her side for many a year now. I am confident that if I offer myself, they will halt their advance."

"I fear this not to be the case," I tell him. "I think there is something deep within the forest that Morgana wants, a sword with considerable power. A weapon that I believe, if she were able to get her hands on, would truly make her unstoppable."

"Maybe by offering myself, she will let our people go." Vireo remains absolute in his plan.

"No!" Killian calls. "I will not allow that to happen. If you offer yourself in surrender, then so do I."

"And I"

"Me too."

"You're not sacrificing yourself, Vireo."

Voices call one at a time, shouting out over one another, all of them with the same tone, with the same message. These people will not allow Vireo to sacrifice himself.

"If that is how you will it, then we stay and we fight." Vireo would be forgiven for feeling overwhelmed by the situation, but I am amazed to see him come into his own, to speak with his people, to only take action or make a decision once they have decided as a group.

"We have been fortifying Verusha in case of such occasions, we have points where those that are too young or too frail to fight can hide until all this is done," Killian says.

"So that is it, then. Those that want to fight and defend our land are welcome to do so. Those who wish to leave for Levanthria, I suggest you make haste and gather as much distance as you can in the time that we have."

There is a raucous cheer amongst the villagers and Vireo leaps from the table onto the ground. "The fight that is about to come to our doorstep is not one we must face for Askela, or Levanthria. It is for us. And for as long as I live, that is something I swear I will always fight for."

The cheers continue, Vireo's words resonating with me. I can only hope that we will be able to defend ourselves against the attack.

Through the swelling group in front of us, Laith emerges, his eyes carrying a look of guilt.

"It is I who caused this situation," he says. "Had I not sent the message to Orjan, he would not have known this camp's whereabouts. I was not prepared to see the hatred that he carries in his heart for Vireo, the shame he showed for myself."

"Trouble yourself no longer, Laith. What is done is done. These people are prepared to fight for their new home, and I intend to help them. Do they have your sword?"

"That goes without saying, Jordell. I will do whatever I can to protect them, whether that costs me my own life. I do still hold hope that Orjan will see sense and do the right thing, I can only hope the darkness that is in his heart lifts and he can see clearly."

"If Orjan brings Morgana and her focus to the boundaries of this forest, then I fear for the path he has chosen to walk. Of the lives that will be lost as a direct consequence of his choices. For that, he will need to be held to account." I take hold of my staff and stand taller than I feel I have for a long time.

"If I could just get through to him, maybe I could get him to see sense, I do not believe Orjan to be a bad person." Laith clings on to his hopes in desperation.

"Laith, you need to understand that if you meet on the

battlefield, you cannot hesitate. To do so only serves to put yourself at greater risk."

"If our paths cross in battle, then I will do what I must."

"Come, we have much to do if we are to be ready for what is to come." The chances of coming out of this battle fare greatly against us, but I have faith in the gods and the fight that they are about to lead us into. I lead Laith to the side, the camp's attention readying for the battle that is to come.

"What is it?" he asks. "We have much to do to ready ourselves for battle."

"How is your shoulder?" I ask.

"I can still wield a sword if that is what you are worried about."

"Does the pain worsen?

"Yes, but it won't stop me from fighting. I will not allow it."

"Show me," I demand, pressing my hand into Laith's shoulder.

"Ow!" Laith slaps my hand away. "What are you doing?" He lowers his tunic and I see that the darkened area is tracking outwards much like the veins in my hand were.

"It is as I feared." I press one hand into his shoulder and concentrate my healing magic, gripping my staff tightly with my other hand. The wood from the Elder Tree pulsates through my arms and down to my palm. The tracked veins retreat backwards before slowly fading, leaving only purple, scarred tissue from the blast.

"How are you doing that?" he asks, a look of wonderment in his eyes.

"Queen Zariah gifted me this staff. It is crafted from the Elder Tree, whose roots created this entire forest."

"Wow."

I look the staff over, admiring the twisted wood the branch has formed naturally, and I wonder how old this branch is. "It has its limits but for the main part, it allows me to cast a more powerful, harnessed variation of my magic, without the same effects on my body that we are used to seeing."

Laith rubs his shoulder and beams. "It is as if it is back to normal. Tell the queen thank you from me."

"When all this is done, you can thank her yourself. Now, we have a battle to get ready for."

34

LAITH

You could cut the tension with a knife. The battle lines are drawn and an eery silence befalls us in the forest. Everyone is in position, exactly where we need them to be, the young and older folk well hidden in safety. Even if we fall here today, at least they will survive. Yaelor, Vireo, Jordell, Killian, and I remain in the main camp, waiting in tense apprehension for our enemies to arrive. A knot forms tightly in my stomach, my hand gripped to the hilt of my blade which remains bound to my waist.

"There is no turning back now," Vireo says. "We have done all that we can."

"I am proud to fight beside you, Vireo, it has been an honour," Killian tells him.

Vireo grins. "Less of that talk. We will continue to fight side by side when all of this is done. And then we are going to drink ourselves into oblivion."

"I will toast to that!" Killian roars with laughter. "Now, where are those bastards?"

"Do you feel ready for what is about to come?" Jordell asks me, a rare look of worry in his aged eyes.

"As ready as I can be," I reply. Jordell readies to leave, his role being to lead the second line of defence within the forest. "Jordell," I call out to him, and he stops in his tracks. "You have done much for me over these years. I hope to show you today just what I have learned from you."

"You are a brave man, Laith. I have no doubt that you will play a big part in what is to come if we are to be victorious. That I am certain of."

"Thank you." I look at him from beneath my brow. "I have never told you how thankful I am for your guidance. I have grown under your watch and all that I am is down to travelling with you. I never knew who my father was, and I guess what I am trying to say is —"

"That is a conversation for another time," Jordell says, a wry smile forming at the side of his mouth. "I have much that I will say to you when all this is done. Just know that I am proud of the man you have become. We are not saying our goodbyes now. I will see you after."

Jordell waves us off and disappears into the trees, and the apprehension of what is to come settles over me like the creeping cold of night frost. No sooner does he leave do I feel the draw of the forest, the silence making it feel more haunted, more secluded than I have ever known it to be. Morning light pierces through above.

"Well, well, well." The broad voice is unmistakable, and anger rushes over me in a way that I was not expecting.

"Lek!" I spit.

No sooner do I mutter his wretched name does the beast emerge from the trees, his green tunic embellished with the symbol of a bear with two axes above it. His eyes are wide like a starving man that is about to devour a feast. He may as well lick his lips in anticipation, he appears that ravenous. He is surrounded by Askelan guards bearing the familiar black and gold tunics and armour. As soon as I see him, bile rises to the back of my throat and I am consumed by a swell of emotions like a rising tide.

"You fucking coward!" Vireo draws his bow and takes aim at him. "If it was not for the fact that I want to savour your death, your body would be laced with arrows."

"Ah, Vireo," Lek glowers. "Lower your bow, you fool. It is not you that we have come for." His gaze darts from Vireo to fix on me, his eyes more feral than I have ever seen them.

"There is no need for you all to die on this day," he announces. "I come with an offer from Morgana. One that I think you would be foolish not to hear." He stands confidently before us, his great axe still strapped to his back.

"Speak!" Vireo barks, his arms tense with the arrow he has drawn in his bow.

"Morgana was visited by Orjan."

My heart drops at the mention of his name, my worst fears realised. Orjan has betrayed us. "What of it!" I call, my hand gripped tightly to the hilt of my blade.

"See, Morgana has had us scouring all of Levanthria looking for you, Laith. The question is, just what is it that she seeks?" Lek raises a giant hand to his thick beard and ruffles it as though thinking, his stony eyes remaining fixated on me.

My mind races. What could Morgana want with me?

"Laith? What role does he have in this?" Vireo asks, his fingers twitching as if he is ready to release his bow at any moment. "Tell me what she wants with him!"

"Do you think that is something she would share with me? Morgana does not share her plans, but what she offers is certainly interesting. Give me the boy and this bloodshed need not happen."

"If this is true, why is Orjan not with you? Why is he not here to claim me?" I demand as my frustration flows like lava cascading down a mountain hill. I draw my sword and point it towards our enemy. "ANSWER ME!"

"When Orjan came to us, he was angry, even angrier than when he first saw me standing by Morgana's side. His hatred for myself and Vireo is incomparable. He offered to bring Vireo to her, and all he asked was that a man named Laith was not harmed," he sneers, still rooted to the spot. "That was when things got interesting. You see, Morgana is not interested in you and even less so in this camp, Vireo. But I saw the blood drain from her skin when she realised *you* were so close." He nods towards me.

"So that's it, you want a trade," I fire back. "I come with you, and these people go free."

"Nearly right. She demands you be executed on this day. Allow this to happen, and no more blood needs to be shed on this day. It's a shame Orjan didn't agree with the plan."

"If it will stop blood from being shed on this day then I give myself freely," I answer, resheathing my sword and stepping forward.

"Laith, no!" Yaelor calls after me. "You can't allow your life to be taken in this way. Something is not right with all this! Why would Morgana be fixated on you?"

Vireo draws his bow further, his aim still steady on Lek. "Regardless of Yaelor's family ties, this does not change anything," he says. "I agree with Yaelor. If Morgana is after you, if she wants you near her, there is a reason for this that we do not yet understand. And I do not draw any comfort from that."

Vireo's jaw is clenched tightly, but he remains in full control of his anger. "We will not allow Laith to sacrifice his life. In these lands, we would lay down our lives to protect each other. The fact that Morgana wishes him dead has shown a weakness, one that we did not know before. She fears him."

Lek roars with laughter. "I was hoping you would say that." He reaches for his great axe, heaving it over his hulking frame. The edges of the axe are stained with blood, and he callously brings it up to his face and sniffs it deeply. "Still smells of Gillam," he sneers.

Before he has chance to do anything else, Vireo releases his own battle roar and his arrow. It buries itself deep into Lek's shoulder, causing him to stagger back. He snaps the arrow that protrudes from his flesh as if it caused him barely any harm, then raises his axe wildly into the air.

"Attack!"

Black and gold colours emerge from the trees, their numbers many, but they are unable to create a formation because of the trees. This is why we chose this point to wait for them; it was part of our plan. I greet the first soldier, drawing my sword across his stomach, his blood the first to be spilled. As much as I wish to allow Morgana to have her way and my life taken, I agree with Vireo. There is much more at play here. Another soldier draws close, but he is dispatched by an arrow that slams into his face.

"Back here, Laith!" Killian yells. Yaelor stands with them, her hatchets in front of her. Killian and Vireo rain down arrows at the soldiers scurrying through the trees, their numbers growing with every passing moment. We dive for cover behind a hut as their own bowmen send across a wave of arrows that decorates the trees around us.

"What now?" Killian asks.

"Wait for our moment." Vireo grins, and I am confused as to what has caught him in such good spirits. He raises his hands to form around his mouth and howls into the trees as though he is possessed by some creature. He continues to howl loudly until we are greeted with even louder howls.

In a moment, wild wolfaires descend on the soldiers, large blurs of fur of varying colours piling into our attackers. The cries of snarls and growls are replaced with the terrified screams of the men and women they tear from limb to limb. Blood soaks the dirt and the leaves as the wolfaires show no mercy to those who encroach on the forest.

"Hold firm!" Lek screams above the chaos. With a mighty swing, he slams his axe into a wolfaire that feasts on a soldier in front of him. It yelps as it falls, panting heavily before Lek swings his great axe once more, drawing a final breath from our defender.

"Go, we need to fall back whilst they are distracted!" Vireo commands. He and Killian step from behind the hut and provide us cover under a flurry of arrows. We set off into the trees but not without a parting gift.

Vireo whistles and the wolfaires stop their assault, disappearing back into the trees where they pounced from. I swing my sword, hacking at a rope that we have bound around the trees. Yaelor does the same on the other side of Killian and Vireo.

A thunderous rumble erupts around us as the earth beneath us begins to shake. It catches me by surprise, and I almost lose my footing, but Killian grabs me by the scruff of my neck just in time. Trunks of felled trees roll down the hill that we climb, tearing up the earth as it forms a deadly trap for those below. Screams of agonised pain reach us as arrows continue to spray in our direction.

We continue up the hill to the next stage of our defence. I hope Jordell is ready for what is about to follow us.

35

JORDELL

"For twelve days and eleven nights the Lords and Baroness' of Levanthria argued and negotiated terms between themselves. Offering one another certain lands and titles if they were to be nominated to ascend the throne. On the twelfth day Lady Morgana attended, without invite and with the briefest of displays of power, two lords and one baroness lost their lives. By the end of the meeting the rest of the parties present agreed that it would be Lady Morgana who would be nominated to become Queen Consort. This decision will have grave consequences for The Great Temple, given that the envoy who attended as a representative was the first to perish by her hands."

AYMARA BLYTHE, *Grand Priestess to the Great Temple, 255 KR*

THE SCREAMS of our attackers send a deep chill down my spine. Their numbers threaten to far outweigh our own. We have picked our point tactically, opting for the high ground of a clearing within the trees, pushing farther beyond the boundaries than we ever have before. I only hope it does not push our newly formed alliance with the fae to the limit.

Part of me hopes that the fae see what is happening, that Queen Zariah is aware of our plight. I have no doubt that if they came to our aid, our safety will be guaranteed.

At the top of the hill, I stand at the front of the line, my staff gripped firmly by my side. There is an air of restlessness about our group, one that I cannot begrudge them. Some have never seen battle but they are willing to take up arms to defend their homes.

From the base of the hill, Laith, Vireo, Killian, and Yaelor emerge at speed. They are sprinting with Killian and Vireo taking it in turns to alternate firing shots into the trees. As they make their way up the hill towards us, I watch them closely, waiting for them to pass the markers that we have set up.

As they do, the first wave of soldiers breaches the trees in pursuit of the others and the sudden realisation of impending battle crashes into me like a battering ram.

I raise my staff into the air and face my comrades. "Today, we fight for our lands. Today, we fight to show them that we will not be pushed around, that we are all free!"

I wait for the Askelan soldiers to start advancing to the foot of the hill. They are unorganised and disjointed. Exactly how we wanted them to be.

"FIRE!" I point my staff down the hill and those in our first row raise their bows into the sky and let loose a flurry of arrows, which dance through the sky in unison before arcing over and dropping down onto our enemy. Bodies drop as the arrows spray over them.

"FIRE!" I call again, and the next row of archers steps forward, raining down another wave of arrows.

Soldiers continue to fall at the foot of the hill, but far-superior numbers continue to advance. We repeat the process, taking out as many of the soldiers as we can as we search to get the upper hand. In the meantime, Laith and the others continue to run toward us.

As the Askelan soldiers advance, their own archers aim up to the heavens and fire arrows. We know from our calculations that their arrows will not reach us, but I fear for the others. Many arrows come dropping down around Laith, Vireo, Killian, and Yaelor, littering the ground around them. It is a game of chance, but I am not about to risk everything by chance.

I raise my staff into the air and draw on a new level of magic I have not experienced. The hairs on my arms stand on edge as magic starts to course through my body and channel into my staff, the tip of which glows as though it is white-hot. As the arrows threaten to end Laith and the others, they snap in the sky, leaving nothing other than a shower of splintered wood as they crash into the largest barrier spell I have ever created. My staff vibrates, emitting a low humming noise as magic enriches the wood. Despite the size and distance of the spell, I do not feel the usual fatigue I endure when casting my magic. I maintain the spell for as long as I need to allow the others the time to reach us. Arrows continue to break as they hit the barrier, landing at various parts of the field.

"What was that?" Killian asks as they reach us.

"My magic grows stronger than it ever has been." I smile. I feel as though there is still much to learn about my newfound strength, my body unburdened from the aftereffects of wielding my power. "I am yet to test how far I can push it."

"Either way, I am grateful for your intervention," Vireo pants as he too reaches us. "I fear that our carcasses would be lined with arrows."

We have little time to converse as the wave of soldiers

descend on us like swarming ants. Our archers continue to fire down on them, but their numbers mean that despite us taking out many, they still outnumber us.

"Get into position!" Vireo calls.

The first row of our defence lays down their bows and kneels on the ground, waiting patiently, their nerves unfettered and inspiring. These men and women fight for each other, every single one of them.

"Hold," Vireo tells them, his focus in the moment of battle.

I stand beside him just behind the first row of people, and Laith and Yaelor take up position, kneeling in front of us.

It doesn't take long for the soldiers to reach us, their weapons drawn, their battle cries reverberating through the air.

"Now!" Vireo commands.

The row in front of them raises wooden pikes which lie dormant on the ground, a death trap for anyone unfortunate enough to run into them.

Bodies slam into the pikes, finding themselves skewered in an instant. Blood sprays everywhere as the Askelan soldiers swarm us. The next wave of their forces is quickly upon us and the close combat begins. I slam my staff against a soldier's chest and as he hits the ground, Yaelor finishes him off, using her hatchets to quickly cleave into his chest with brutal efficiency.

Metal clashes against metal as the sound of battle and subsequent death begins to echo across the lands.

Our fighters hold their ground well, and although I see one or two fall, the Askelan troops are losing more men. The high ground is working. Through the bodies, I see Lek approaching, his battle-axe gripped by both his hands. Its blade drips with the blood of our own and I hear him call out across the battlefield.

"Vireo!" he roars.

Vireo is not one for hiding, and the green blur of his cloak whips past me as he careens down the hill towards his sworn enemy. A soldier swings his sword at him, but I channel my magic and fire a blast of energy into his chest which knocks him to the ground with a thud. Vireo then takes out two more soldiers quickly with his blade, drawing it across one's neck before driving his sword deep into the other's chest.

"Lek!" Vireo dives through the air with his sword outstretched. Lek grins wildly as his former friend approaches him. Vireo is well within the enemy camp, and it is all I can do to keep the soldiers at bay whilst he enters combat with Lek. I fire smouldering blasts of energy from my hand and the end of my staff, and as my magic hails down on our enemies, they drop quickly, my magic searing into their skin. Lek raises his axe on its side, holding it above him as Vireo brings his sword down. There is a spark as the two weapons collide and they begin their fight, both faces snarling with hatred as each tries to best the other.

Soldiers continue to push up the hill towards us, vastly outnumbering us. As they continue to swarm us, my brain starts to search for answers on how we can defeat our invading enemies.

Laith and Yaelor continue to battle from the front, taking down multiple soldiers as they fight side by side with impressive speed and efficiency. However, I fear how long this can be maintained with more soldiers advancing on us.

I stare down the hill at the swarm approaching and realise that if they reach us, this battle will quickly be over. It appears that Lek's battle plan is to simply outnumber us.

I start to draw on my magic, the tip of my staff glowing whiter than ever. It vibrates so wildly that I struggle to keep hold of it. Then I feel a connection to the staff itself, and a strange sense of reassurance comes over me as if the staff itself guides me. I let the power in, slamming my staff into the ground and drawing on the energy of the forest. Crackles of energy flow from the ground and into my staff before coursing through my arms and into the rest of my body. I do not feel pain or discomfort for the levels of power that I draw. In fact, it is quite the opposite. My body feels invigorated and energised as I embrace the magic that my staff lets me draw upon.

My clothes ruffle as wildly as my hair as though I stand in the centre of a storm. Some of the soldiers stop in their tracks, faces filled with panic. I raise my staff from the ground before putting all my power into my spell, embracing every essence of the magic that tracks through my skin. Slamming my staff into the ground, I let out an almighty roar whilst focusing my spell halfway down the hill. The ground shakes aggressively, fighters from both sides losing their footing. As I focus my spell, I barely notice the blade that is driving towards my head, but Laith's sword intervenes to block this before he strikes down the soldier.

The ground continues to rumble, interrupting the immediate battle around us before I allow a blast of energy to pulse into the hill. As the ground shakes, the earth cracks below us further down the hill and it triggers a landslide. A wall of earth and stone forces itself down the hill, devouring the many troops that were making their way towards us. It is impossible to fight such a force, and their numbers quickly shrink as the soldiers meet their ends, crushed and buried alive.

I continue the spell for as long as I can, my magic rippling around me until a sharp sting greets my hand. I take the pain as a warning from my staff, Queen Zariah having advised me of the consequences should I push my magic too far. I pull back, allowing the energy to disperse and severing my connection to the ground as quickly as I can, fearing that the surge could break my staff. My body is tired from the spell, but the usual eruption of agony does not engulf my body. I am fatigued but not hindered by my magic-use.

We have gained a strong advantage, but those not crushed by my magical landslide continue to climb the disfigured terrain towards us. My attention spins to Lek and Vireo who remain locked in combat with one another, oblivious to the carnage around them as if it is only them on the battlefield. The two exchange blows with Vireo's speed matched by Lek's strength. Lek wields his axe with brutal precision. He aims a wild boot at Vireo which connects with his chest, flooring him in an instant. Vireo gasps, his eyes wide. Lek raises his axe, ready to bring it down on Vireo. Before I have chance to draw on my magic, Laith throws himself at Lek, catching him off guard. The two of them roll down the hill, Lek dropping his axe in the process. Furious, Lek appears to regain his composure as he climbs above a sprawling Laith and thunders fists down on his chest.

I fire a blast of energy into Lek's back, forcing him from Laith. He stares us down, his face bloody, his body heaving for air.

"Four against one?" he glowers, standing tall, ready to fight all of us. Vireo, Yaelor, Laith, and I stand side by side, ready to strike him down. It is no less than he deserves.

Lek is undeterred, however, and grins wildly as if it is he who has the upper hand. He reaches inside his tunic and removes an elixir.

"Stop him quickly!" I yell, knowing full well the power such dark potions will allow him.

Vireo looks puzzled by my panic, but Yaelor and Laith understand why we need to disarm him. They drive towards him at speed as Lek draws the potent elixir to his lips, emptying its contents into his mouth.

36
LAITH

We are not quick enough to reach Lek before he consumes the elixir in an instant. He roars in pain, his face contorted, his eyes bulging from the fae magic that courses through his veins. Yaelor is faster than me and swipes at him with her hatchets. Lek steps into her space, slamming his shoulder into her. With a sickening crunch, she stops dead in the air before crashing to the ground, her weapons sent sprawling from her grip. One of the hatchets launches into the air and as I am unarmed, I take my opportunity to grab it as I bear down on Lek. I jump through the air towards him but his speed shocks me as he turns and sends his boulder-like fist into my chest.

All the air leaves me in an instant, and I slide through the blood-soaked grass only stopping when I roll into a dead soldier. I gasp, desperately trying to breathe, but I can't take in any air. My ribs burn and ache with tremendous pain and I know straight away that he has likely broken my ribs. As I take in short, sharp breaths, it feels as though daggers pierce my side and I cough and wheeze as I recover from the blow. In a flash, Lek has taken out two more men, the elixir he drank seemingly increasing his speed and strength. His veins protrude as he stands roaring in anger and pain, allowing the elixir to consume him, a magic force whipping up the air around him. I desperately try to claw at the ground to allow myself to stand and fight alongside Vireo and Jordell, but the pain in my ribs causes my arms to buckle.

"VIREO!" Lek yells, his energy growing even stronger. His muscles seem to grow before us, his bones cracking with the strain the magic puts on his body.

Vireo quickly removes his bow and fires an arrow at Lek, but he moves at such speed that the arrow misses. Lek snarls and starts covering ground at an alarming rate as he charges towards Vireo. Vireo quickly fires what looks to be his last arrow, and as Lek reaches him, it embeds into his shoulder. Lek barely notices this as he swings his fist at Vireo who uses his arms to brace the blow. With a snap, Vireo howls as his left arm breaks from the force of the blow. Had that blow connected with his head or body, it would have surely ended him. I move towards them as quickly as I can.

Lek grabs hold of Vireo's collar and heaves him up from the ground, drawing him towards his snarling face. His eyes are wide and bulging as Lek slams his head into Vireo's nose, tossing him to the ground like a ragdoll. Vireo lies in a crumpled heap, unconscious from the attack, his face covered in blood and his arm sitting at an unnatural angle.

With a whack, Jordell's staff bounces of the back of Lek's head. This only seems to anger him more. Lek turns and stands taller than ever before, his hulking frame dwarfing that of Jordell. Jordell does not show any signs of intimidation as he fires his magic into Lek's chest, but Lek remains unmoved.

A strange noise rings in my ears, like metal resonating at a high pitch. The noise causes me to wince, stopping me in my tracks, and I feel a deep pressure within my head. Is this a consequence of my blow? Am I concussed? I draw my hand to my face and it turns red as crimson blood drips from my nose. The noise gets louder, and I call out in pain, panicked and confused.

"Laith," a voice hisses. Unknown to me, has the blow driven me to madness? "I can help you. I can help you end this." The voice calls to me, causing me to search the immediate area around me to find the source.

"Keep looking!" The voice is charming, yet tainted with pain. My eyes dart around until I see a stone protruding from the ground that Jordell turned over with his magic.

"There!" the voice calls. "Head to the stone!"

Confused, I drag myself from the ground. "I can help you, Laith. You can end all of this!" Jordell continues to pepper Lek with magic whilst keeping his distance as best as he can. Jordell's mobility and speed surprise me, as I have never seen him move in such a way. He holds his own for now against Lek, but my fear for how long he can maintain this pushes to the forefront of my mind.

"Move, Laith, unless you want to see those you hold closest perish!" There is a rushed urgency to the voice that calls over to me. "Move to the stone!"

I stagger forward as directed, navigating the rocky, uneven terrain underfoot.

"Hurry!" the voice cries in a frustrated tone.

I reach the stone, a section of which protrudes from the ground, confused as to how this stone will help me with the fight.

I stare blankly at the stone. "This is madness," I mutter to myself.

"QUICKLY!" The voice is more aggressive this time, desperate.

Ignoring the pain in my side, I drop to my knees and start shovelling away the dirt with my hands as fast as I can. After only a few moments, my fingers hit against what I assume to be the bottom half of the stone. That is, until the glint of gold catches the light.

"That's it, that is what you are searching for."

I claw out the rubble as fast as I can, one eye on Jordell and Lek.

"Faster." A sense of anticipation and excitement on the voice.

As I remove the dirt, I am surprised to see the hilt of a sword protruding from the stone, a red jewel encrusted into the base of the hilt.

"Grab the sword, it can help you defeat your enemies," the voice vows.

I grab hold of the hilt and pull on the blade, but it remains embedded in the stone, unmoving.

"Concentrate, I can help you end this."

I pull on the sword again, but the blade seems to weigh more than the rock itself. I raise my head to see Jordell dodging Lek's attempts to strike him. Although Jordell is wielding magic far stronger than I have ever seen from him, Lek is faster and stronger from the elixir. Jordell raises his staff to create a barrier spell but Lek breaks this and grips hold of Jordell with one hand before striking him with the other. Jordell's head snaps back and Lek throws him to the ground.

"Jordell!" I cry, setting off to help him. Our numbers decline, as do the guards that we fight, combat still raging on between our two forces. Blood soaks into the green terrain where we fight, blemishing this once-tranquil area, forever tainted by our war.

"Stop! You will only succeed with this sword! Release me!"

I don't process the words fully. Dread overcoming me, I

pull on the sword, desperately hoping that this is not simply madness that consumes me. I feel slight movement that grants me hope. As it moves, I feel a surge of energy rise through my arms from the hilt of the blade. It is like nothing I have ever felt before, the euphoric sensation exploding into my body, into my mind. I continue to pull on the hilt with a newfound will to remove it, to protect Jordell and the others from this monster.

"Yes, that's it!" the voice hisses, excited by my actions.

I put everything I have into pulling on the blade. With a final heave, it glides out from within the stone, and I stagger backwards. I have no idea where this blade came from, but my confidence grows, and I feel stronger and rejuvenated as if I have not been fighting at all. I wield the sword just in time as Lek now moves towards a heavily dazed Jordell, his great axe gripped in one hand. He raises it, ready to kill him. I launch myself towards him, surprised by my own speed. As Lek brings his axe downward, I thrust the sword up to protect Jordell. Despite Lek's far-superior strength, his weapon remains in the air as I draw on my strength to block the attack. His eyes widen in shock at the intervention, confused by how I can hold my own against his hulking frame. I grit my teeth and push back against him, forcing some distance between us. Lek roars in anger and swings at me again with a berserker-style rage, but I stop him again, blocking the attack before pushing him back once more.

"How – how do you do this?" he roars, swinging his axe continuously towards me, the speed of which is impressive. Each blow I find I block with ease, barely straining, barely affected by the impact. Each failed strike only serves to increase Lek's rage, his muscles bulging to the point where it looks like his skin will tear.

"Let me guide you!" the voice enters my mind, this time

accompanied by a stinging pain in the centre of my forehead. "I can help you end this, let me in."

The power of the blade flows through me and my confidence increases in an instant, a surge of energy flowing around me and the blade that I wield.

"Is that all you have, Lek?" I tease. "I am disappointed." Ahead of me, Killian and a group of our fighters fend off the dwindling numbers of the Askelan guards, the sight of which only fuels my confidence.

Lek's face seems to implode on itself.

"You will pay for what you did to Gillam." I offer him a sly smirk. "How does it feel to be bested by a boy?"

"Bested!" he rages. "You know nothing of the magic you face!" Lek places his hand into his tunic and removes another vial of black elixir. He gulps it down like a babe suckling a breast, then drops to his knees as the unnatural force engulfs him. He roars in pain, the whites of his eyes vanishing, his pupils turning completely black. The elixir has made him feral, his anger getting the better of his decisions. A valuable lesson I learned from Vireo.

Lek charges at me, enraged and out of control. I dive out of the way as he swings his axe at me, which is close enough that I feel the air push past me. As he spins, he threatens to cleave me in half, but I raise my sword to my side to block him. He presses against me, his hot, snarling breath close enough for me to feel it against my face. I remove my sword quickly, catching him off balance with my speed, then drive the sword upwards, removing Lek's arm from just below his elbow.

With a howl of pain, he staggers backwards, his blackened blood spraying everywhere around him.

He gapes at me with hatred and I ready myself for his next move, having now gained the upper hand. It does not happen, however; with a crunch, his right eye explodes as an arrow embeds into his skull.

"That one was for Gillam!" Vireo yells from over my shoulder.

Lek staggers backwards, but is still moving somehow, and another arrow quickly fires into his chest. Lek roars a blood-curdling battle cry, enraged. Not wanting to give him any time, I rush towards him at speed and am quickly upon him. I roar in anger as I put everything into my final blow, hoping that his final few moments have been in excruciating pain. It is no less than he deserves. As I spin, I detach his head from his shoulders. It bounces onto the blood-filled ground, mouth agape.

The remaining Askelan soldiers see sense and begin their retreat into the forest, to the wild cheers of those of our camp who remain. We have suffered heavy losses, but we live to fight another day.

It is done. The battle is over. Somehow, we have bested them.

I rush to Jordell and offer my hand to help him from the ground. He is dazed, and after a few moments of his eyes searching wearily at his surroundings, he notices the sword that I hold.

"Where did you get that?" he asks in wonderment.

"I will sound like a madman when I explain."

"I care not where you got it, how was it you were able to match Lek's strength with it?" Vireo asks.

"This is the sword we have been searching for, the one that I have foreseen in my vision. This sword, it holds the key to ending this war. To bringing better times to Levanthria," Jordell breathes, staring in wonderment at the weapon.

"I prefer chaos." The words leave my mouth to my own surprise, words I did not intend to speak. The sharpened pain returns to my mind, causing me to wince. What is this witchcraft that befalls me? My arm rises in front of me as though inspecting a new limb, but I am not in control of the movement.

"What's happening?" I attempt to ask, but the words do not leave my lips, and a panic overcomes me. It is as though my consciousness is being pressed to the back of my mind. I try to scream but nothing happens as my body continues to talk and move without my say-so. The searing pain in my head worsens. I try to fight back but the pain engulfs my mind the harder I try.

A blackness greets me, and I am left suspended in a void.

37

JORDELL

"Long live Queen Morgana, may she bring a new age to Levanthria."

255 KR

"CHAOS?" I ask, confused by Laith's words. "Why would you enjoy chaos?" Maybe he has taken one too many blows to the head.

"Through chaos," Laith says, "there is order." There is something different about Laith, something that I do not like that causes alarm. He carries himself differently, his eyes narrowing, a wry smile on his face. "For thousands of years I have been trapped, but thanks to your friend, I find myself free and able to walk these lands once more." Laith looks around at our surroundings in amazement. "Although things look a little different from last time I was here."

"The sword," I say. It is the only thing I can think of. "You're – "

"Rhagor?" he answers, cutting my words short.

Laith stands before me, but it is as though I am greeted by a stranger, the way he holds himself is different, more arrogant. His eyes are narrower, his eyebrows bowed, an uncharacteristic sneer on his curt lips.

"What have you done with Laith?" I ask, panic threatening to overcome me.

For a moment no words are exchanged, and I simply stand and stare down the god that stands before me. "Answer me!" I roar.

"I answer to no man!" Rhagor bellows back, his face twisting with anger. "You are in the presence of a god, and you will bow before me."

"What have you done with the person who that body belongs to?" I demand, unmoving in my focus.

Rhagor rolls his eyes whilst gripping the hilt of his sword, the tip of which is pressed lightly into the sodden ground. "This body, it is young and strong, perfect for me." He raises one of his hands and inspects it closely before offering me a patronising smile. "It feels good to be free of the stone prison my mother deemed suitable for me. I think I will hold onto this body."

"What of Laith!" I scream, fearing the worst.

"Think of his consciousness as being imprisoned. He can have his body back when I am done with it. Whether his mind will be able to process everything he sees in the future is another thing." His grin is wide, and a fury rises within me.

"You are no god, you are a monster," I growl, my knuckles whitening as I grip my staff.

"Insolence! You will show your god more respect than this!" Rhagor's knuckles crack as he squeezes his sword tightly.

"You are not our god!" Vireo cries as he moves by my side. He is being supported to stand by Yaelor.

"Brave words from a peasant," Rhagor snarls, ripping the sword up out of the ground. Within a moment, powerful energy engulfs him, whipping a frenzied storm up from the ground. Leaves, dirt, branches, and splashes of blood swirl around us as Rhagor draws on his power. It takes my breath away and it takes every part of my strength to simply remain standing. I plant my feet to the ground, just about managing to keep my balance. I have never felt power like this. As his energy grows and grows, his eyes widen as if he is invigorated by the power surge.

"You will kneel before me!" Rhagor demands. He points a finger at me before swinging his sword, and a blast of magic fires towards us, larger than anything I have ever seen before.

My staff glows brightly as it draws on energy from the forest of its own accord, as if controlled by someone else. I feel the magic rise from the ground and pulsate into my arms, my body tensing up as the power courses through me. It is as though I am a conduit for the staff instead of the other way around. My own thoughts become guided as if my instinct tells me what to do. I step towards the blast and spin into it, greeting the magic with the side of my staff as I send the magic back towards Rhagor.

His face drops in surprise at my action and as I threaten to turn his own magic against him, he uses his sword to deflect the blast away from himself and towards the trees behind him. When it hits them, it tears through the trunks, sending multiple trees crashing to the ground, an army of birds escaping from the foliage.

This quickly turns to rage as Rhagor fixes his stern gaze on Vireo and Yaelor who stand beside me. He swings his blade quickly, firing three further blasts towards them. The magic is ferocious and sears the ground as it approaches them, the heat threatening to sear our skin, even at this distance.

I step in front of the blasts and slam my staff into the ground, letting the forest's magic guide me once more. It flows freely through my body. I feel the strain given the amount of energy being used, but it is a level I can sustain.

The blasts explode in front of us as if they have been met by a wall of glass, my barrier spell sustaining the refined power that Rhagor wields. The blast causes me to stagger back as molten magic lashes against the ground in front of us once it disperses. Had that blast connected, it would have incinerated all three of us.

"That is not possible!" Rhagor inspects his sword as if it is broken. "How is it you have my sister's blessing?" he asks. "It was my killing of her that led to me being entombed in stone for all this time. How is it that you wield her magic? I sense it, I can feel it." He takes an over-exaggerated inhale of air through his nose. "I can smell her power, this place reeks of it." His eyes light up as they are drawn to the staff that I wield, my own artefact. "How does it feel to wield the power of a god?" he asks.

I have never thought about it this way.

"I do not have time for this." Rhagor raises his head and calls out as if talking to the whispering winds that swirl towards the trees. "Sister, you have chosen your champion. It will be interesting to see how all of this plays out." Rhagor smiles at me, then raises his sword and slams it into the ground. With a flash, he is gone, his whereabouts unknown.

"No, it can't be. This is not what the vision showed me." I feel numb. The sword was meant to bring about an age of prosperity. Instead, it has released the fury of a god long trapped, seeking vengeance on these lands. I cannot bear the thought of what has happened to Laith, my dear Laith. My legs buckle at the knees.

"What have I done?" I desperately search the skies above, looking for the answers to the many questions I have. "Why have you twisted my visions to bring us to this point?" I scream at the gods who clearly toy with me. "Why is it you manipulate us in such ways?"

Laith is gone. His kindness, his bravery, taken in an instant by a god who cares not for his body.

"What the fuck was that?" Vireo asks. "Jordell, JORDELL!" Vireo knocks against my shoulder, his words a mere dampness in my periphery. "If it is true what he says and he is in fact a god, we are not equipped to fight him. We barely made it out alive against the Askelan forces."

Vireo is true in what he says. I have dedicated my life for the last few years to finding that blade. I was so sure that it would end the Great War that is to come, but instead it seems to be the trigger. All that we have done, everything we have been through, we were just playing right into the hands of fate.

"I – I don't know what to do." I drop my staff to the ground and raise my trembling hands to my face.

"What about Laith? There has to be a way to get him back," Yaelor asks, panic-stricken, showing a rare glimpse of her emotion.

"I don't know, Yaelor. He is gone. My son, he is gone." Tears erupt, stinging my eyes. My chest feels as though it is about to collapse on itself. Each breath is heavy as I gasp for air, grief eviscerating any other emotion in my body.

"He was supposed to bring about the change needed in this world," I splutter. And for the first time, I am bereft of any ideas. I have no answers.

How does one go to war with a god?

FIND OUT WHAT HAPPENED TO THE KING

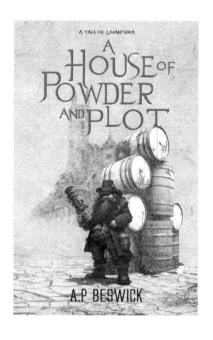

All will be revealed in A House Of Powder And Plot, A Tale Of Levanthria - Out November 5th 2023.

ALSO BY A.P BESWICK

OTHER BOOKS IN THE LEVANTHRIA SERIES

A Forest Of Vanity And Valour

A Sea Of Sorrow And Scorn

A Kingdom Of Courage and Cruelty

A Frost Of Fear And Fortitude

A Loch Of Grace And Greed - Free Short Story Dust - Free Short Story

Coming Soon And Available For Pre-Order

A House Of Powder And Plot

A Frost Of Death And Deceit

A Forest Of Bastards And Betrayal

A War Of Chaos And Fury

JOIN MY NEWSLETTER

I hope you enjoyed this story. If you would like to keep up to date with my books as well as read one of my free short stories you can do

so by joining my newsletter HERE or visiting www.apbeswick.com

Made in the USA
Columbia, SC
02 August 2024

3b3da33a-0ab2-4cd5-bf1e-c5fb6085f014R01